W9-AVK-191

CHRISTMAS IN SUGARCREEK

Also by Shelley Shepard Gray

Sisters of the Heart series

HIDDEN
WANTED
FORGIVEN
GRACE

Seasons of Sugarcreek series

WINTER'S AWAKENING
SPRING'S RENEWAL
AUTUMN'S PROMISE

Families of Honor

THE CAREGIVER
THE PROTECTOR
THE SURVIVOR

CHRISTMAS IN SUGARCREEK

A Christmas Seasons in Sugarcreek Novel

SHELLEY SHEPARD GRAY

Doubleday Large Print
Home Library Edition

INSPIRE

An Imprint of HarperCollins*Publishers*

This Large Print Edition, prepared especially for Doubleday Large Print Home Library, contains the complete, unabridged text of the original Publisher's Edition.

ISBN 978-1-61793-241-0

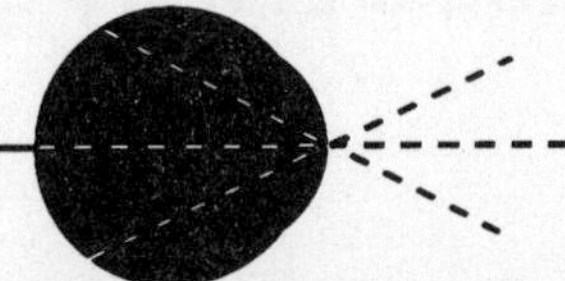

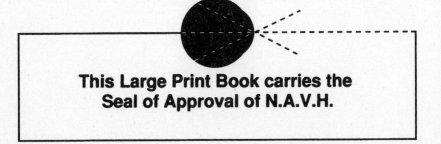

This Large Print Book carries the Seal of Approval of N.A.V.H.

To Pastor Jonathan Eilert, for preaching a sermon that inspired a book.

To my Huddle girlfriends, Rosann, Kara, Judi, Janice, and Pat. Thank y'all for being my light.

When Jesus spoke again to the people, He said, “I am the light of the world. Whoever follows me will never walk in darkness, but will have the light of life.”

John 8:12

The woods would be silent if only the best birds sang.

~Amish proverb

CHRISTMAS IN SUGARCREEK

Chapter One

Ten Days Until Christmas

"Judith, are you sure you don't mind locking up tonight?" asked Joshua, a guilty tone heavy in his voice. "I feel bad, letting you close the store two nights in a row."

"You shouldn't. I don't mind staying late at all. That's what sisters are for, *jah*?"

When Josh continued to look doubtful, Judith Graber lifted her chin, forced a smile she didn't feel inside. "Come, now. Gretta needs you. As does Will. Go on, or you're going to be late. You two have plans, don'tcha?"

"Nothing much. We're just getting together for supper with some other couples. You know, before things get too busy."

She knew Joshua was talking about Christmas get-togethers and other holiday parties. Every *frau* she knew was busy baking and cooking for the planned activities.

Being single, she was not. "Go now, Joshua. I'll be fine."

"I promise, I'll close the rest of the week," he said as he shrugged on his coat.

Judith crossed her arms over her chest. "You better," she teased with a mock frown.

However, she doubted her *bruder* had even noticed her expression. He was already beyond the wreath-adorned door that was closing behind him with a jangling of bells.

Judith watched through the store's large picture windows as her brother weaved in between two parked cars and then, reaching the sidewalk, almost knocked into a woman carrying a wrapped package. He was practically racing home.

To his new home.

Just two months ago, he and Gretta had told the whole family that they were moving into a small house two blocks from the store.

Living above the family shop no longer made sense, especially with Gretta in a family way again.

No member of the Graber family disagreed with their decision.

But, of course, none of them had been prepared for the adjustments that would have to be made now that Joshua would no longer be on the premises at all times. Now each member of the family had to take turns opening and closing the shop. Well, she, Joshua, and her father. Mamm was still too busy at home with the little ones to come in much, and Caleb had recently started at the brick factory. Anson was still a little too young to be of any real help.

So, it fell on Judith to do the majority of the work. *As always.*

Because she was the steady one.

The reliable one.

More like the one who had no life, Judith thought wryly. All while Joshua had been falling in love, and her brother Caleb had been struggling with his future, and even as Anson wrestled with his own growing pains, she had held steady and had quietly done what was expected of her.

Everyone was appreciative, to be sure. But that didn't ease the restless ache that seemed to be growing inside.

Wistfully, Judith looked out the window at the gently falling snow, the wheel ruts in the lane, the road beyond that led . . . somewhere else.

She wished that she, like Joshua, had somewhere to run to. Wished she had someone who counted the passing minutes of her absence . . .

If only . . .

Realizing she'd been standing there in a daze, Judith slapped her hands on the counter. "If you're going to be so dreamy, you might as well be truthful about it," she said out loud. "You don't wish just for *someone*. You wish you had a *man, a sweetheart,* counting the minutes until he saw you again."

Her hollow laugh echoed through the empty store, a store that surely needed tending. And she knew from experience that wishes and dreams didn't get things done.

Since there were only five more minutes until closing time, she left her spot behind the counter and began her usual walk through the store. As she did so, she organized stock and picked up stray pieces of trash people had left behind. A child's toy, a gum wrapper. A grocery list.

The bells on the door jingled merrily, causing her to straighten.

"Hello?" a deep voice called out.

Well, of course someone decided to come in, now that it was mere minutes before closing time. Irritation flowed through her as she stood with her hands full of trash and a metal toy car, as the person darted toward the front. "May I help you?" she called out.

Then skidded to a stop. Because right there in front of her was Benjamin Knox.

Recognition flashed in his eyes as he glanced her way. And then a long, slow smile spread. A knowing and too-personal smile. "Judith Graber . . . Hi."

"Ben." She lifted her chin, pretending that she wasn't shocked to her core. Two years ago, Ben Knox had left Sugarcreek under a haze of disapproval. Gossips reported that he'd gone to Missouri to help some cousins on their dairy farm, but had in truth done little besides flirt with the girls.

She needed to remember that. Keeping

her voice cool and even, she asked, "May I help you?"

Under his black hat's thick felt brim, his hazel eyes seemed to take in every inch of her. She felt his gaze's sweep as surely as if he'd run a hand right down her periwinkle dress, down her black apron, along her black stockings.

"Nee," he said.

She couldn't remember what she'd asked him. *"Nee?"*

"No, I don't need your help," he said with an almost-smirk. "I'm not here for anything special. Just thought I'd look around for a few minutes. You know. See if there was anything that catches my eye."

"And do you think there might be?"

"Doubt it."

Judith went cold. Was he purposely being rude, or was she being too sensitive?

Probably a bit of both.

Keenly aware of the tension she felt around Ben—that bit of unease she'd always felt around him—she cleared her throat. "Just to let you know, we're closing in exactly one minute."

An eyebrow rose. "In one minute, huh?

Then what happens? All customers get locked in?"

"Of course not!" Oh, but of course he was teasing her. "What I meant to say is that you should probably leave."

"Right now? Before I get a chance to look around some more?" He turned around and stared at the clock above the door. The ridiculous clock with birds on the face instead of numbers. The clock that chirped on the hour, much to the amusement of her mother . . . and to her extreme annoyance.

Before she could answer, the clock struck six and chirped. When he grinned, she felt her cheeks heat. Wished she was absolutely anywhere else but here, with him. Alone together in the store.

Ben Knox bit the inside of his cheek to keep from laughing.

It wasn't because of the clock—his Aunt Beth had a large collection of hand-painted birdhouses on a shelf in her kitchen. He was used to such silly items.

No, what had him tempted to laugh was the girl standing across from him. Standing as stiff and looking as ruffled as the clock's fierce mother sparrow painted where the number three would be.

But that was where the similarities ended. Judith Graber was far from being just a difficult, fussy girl, and she was not drab at all. No, her bright blue eyes and lovely light brown hair with its streaks of auburn caught his eye like little else.

He found her exasperation with him amusing. And very little had amused him in a long time.

"I guess the cardinal's trill is my signal to leave?"

Her gaze seemed to give off sparks. *"Jah."*

He turned away, but a nagging question turned him back around.

"Why are you working here so late, and all alone? I would've thought your husband would want you home by now."

"I work here because it's my family's store, of course." After a pause, she looked down at her hands clasping the countertop. "Besides, I'm not married."

She wasn't? A flash of hope exploded inside of him. He tamped it down with effort. "Are you courting?" It was rude of him to ask, but he couldn't help himself.

Raising her chin, Judith's lips pursed, just as if she was searching the air for the right words. At last, she sighed. "*Nee* . . . though it surely isn't any of your business."

Now it was his turn to be surprised. All his life, he'd thought of Judith Graber as being the ideal girl. She was lovely and kind and a hard worker—nothing like himself.

And she was loyal. Vividly, he recalled her standing up for her brothers anytime someone threatened them or put one of them down.

In short, she was the type of girl men like him never spent time with. She was too fine for the likes of Benjamin Knox. She always had been, and everyone knew it.

For the first time, though, the thought made him sad. Like he'd missed his ride and was going to be reduced to waiting on a street corner for another person to pick him up—but no one was approaching.

"Why did you come back to Sugarcreek, Ben Knox?"

"Because it was time," he said, though it really told her nothing. And told himself nothing, too. He'd come back because he was tired of Missouri. And before he lost his nerve, he'd put his house on the market. He was hoping the house would sell fast. It was almost physically hard to be there. Probably most people felt that way about places filled with hurts and bad memories.

When Judith still stared, all bright and beautiful, he forced himself to tell her the truth. Just this once.

"I wanted to come back and have Christmas in Sugarcreek. For one last time."

Her mouth went slack. "For only one last time?"

Because he'd told her too much, because the sudden feeling of loss was much too painful, he winked. "*Jah.* Not that it's any of your business."

With that, he forced himself to turn. Opened the door. Walked right under the chirping bird clock and away from the temptation that was Judith Graber.

The bitter cold that fanned his cheeks felt like heaven.

In spite of her best efforts, she still was a terrible cook, Lilly Miller decided as she pulled the roast chicken out of the oven and set it on the counter. Grimacing, she examined it closely, hoping that under closer scrutiny, things were better than she thought.

They weren't. Without a doubt, she'd burned dinner. Again.

With a sigh, Lilly tugged on a wing. Instead of staying put, it pulled right off, just like it was relieved to be free of the burnt carcass. "I don't blame you, wing," she said out loud. "I'd escape this meal if I could, too. I've managed to ruin yet another dinner. Now what am I going to feed Robert?"

For a moment, she stared at their house phone. It would be so easy to call her mom and ask for cooking help. But her mom was busy with baby Carrie and certainly didn't need Lilly bugging her again.

With a wince, Lilly knew she'd asked her mother for help more times during the last two months than she had for the first eighteen years of her life.

Being married was not for sissies! Though she and Robert had been married for two months now, Lilly was still finding it challenging. First there were the adjustments to be made, living as a Mennonite. Then there were all the challenges of being newlyweds. Especially since she was married to a man who'd been married before—to the perfect woman.

More than any of that, she was finding it difficult to be worthy of a man like Robert. A man who'd given up practically everything for her. After all, she couldn't even roast a chicken properly. Or make decent mashed potatoes.

Or bake his favorite cake.

The fact of the matter was that sometimes when he left for work, Lilly wondered if he was glad to be away from her. She was young and impulsive and sometimes—okay, most of the time—spoke without thinking first.

Anxious for help, she looked longingly at her computer. Ever since she'd left Cleveland and started over in Sugarcreek, she'd become dependent on the thing. She bought music and used it as a stereo. She got on Facebook and stayed connected with the few girlfriends she kept in touch with from high school. She searched for recipes and simple instructions on how to sew her new dresses.

Last week, she'd even looked into the idea of taking some online classes. Though she knew she had little in common with most college coeds, it didn't mean she didn't want to learn anymore.

But each night when Robert came home, she quickly turned off the computer. And of course, she was never going to mention her college idea. After all, Robert sometimes confided that he felt dumber than her—his words not hers—because he only had an eighth-grade education.

He also didn't trust her computer. Though he never said the words, she felt it. Which made her feel even more confused.

Now completely depressed and annoyed with herself, she turned her back on the burnt offering and sat down at the kitchen table. Here it was, ten days before Christmas, and she still had no gift for Robert.

Originally, she'd wanted to try to sew him something, but that had been a hopeless task.

A silly one, too. Robert was enjoying his new jeans and thick flannel shirts.

So she'd decided to make him something—just like he'd promised that he was going to make something for her.

But the problem was, she wasn't crafty. She couldn't sew. Or cook all that well.

Okay. She couldn't cook at all.

As time marched closer to Christmas Day, a small knot of worry in her stomach seemed to grow bigger each day. She needed to make something wonderful for Robert—or get him something special.

Otherwise, she'd have to face the horrible truth: sooner or later, Robert Miller was going to regret marrying her.

As Caleb Graber was walking along the snowy sidewalk, he rolled his neck. Half as an attempt to get the stiffness out of it from lifting dozens of palates of bricks at the factory, and half as an effort to get mentally prepared to see Rebecca.

It was pretty much a fact: he was completely obsessed with Rebecca Yoder.

Of course, there was no way he was going to act too eager to see her. Even he knew that girls didn't like pushy, clingy men. But that's how he felt. Like there wasn't a moment during the day that he didn't want to be with her.

Which took him completely by surprise.

From the first moment he saw her at Mrs. Miller's, Caleb had been eager to see her again. After the year he'd had, constantly feeling part of two worlds but never being a good match in either, the comfort he was feeling from being near Rebecca was a peace he couldn't deny. She always looked at him with acceptance. As if seeing him made her day.

Which was how he felt about her. However, he was afraid he'd scare her off . . . if she knew just how much he felt he needed her, and if she realized that he was thinking about scary things whenever he was around her. Things like courting and marriage.

Marriage! At eighteen!

Even thinking about being married made him woozy. But what scared him far worse—not that it was anyone else's business—was that the thought of being without Rebecca made him feel physically ill.

Therefore, he was just going to have to play it cool. All he really had to do when he was around Rebecca was be kind and respectful. Those were qualities she seemed to appreciate. And those things he could do without letting her know just how crazy he was about her.

With that in mind, he stomped up the snow-covered stairs leading to the library and carefully schooled his features to look cool. Almost bored.

Before he could even open the front door and step inside, Rebecca walked right out. "Hi, Caleb."

Her eyes were bright, her wheat-colored hair as shiny and glossy as ever. And just like that, he gave in and grinned as well. Being "cool" was overrated, anyway. "Hi, Rebecca."

She already had on her black cloak and bonnet. "I hope the walk to the library wasn't too terrible."

"It was fine."

"I didna want you having to wait long, neither. So I'm all ready."

"I wouldn't have minded waiting. And Becca, I wouldn't have minded getting you at your house." In fact, he would have preferred that. There seemed to be something vaguely wrong about never walking her home. Or visiting with her parents, just to show them that he cared about Rebecca enough to always look out for her.

Her smile dimmed. “There was no need for you to go there. This was closer to your work.”

Her words were true, but still Caleb felt awkward. So far, whenever he’d seen her, she had always insisted on meeting him some place in town. It was almost like she never wanted him to see her house.

Or maybe it was that she didn’t want him to meet her family?

“Rebecca, next time, I’ll come get you at your house, okay? I don’t want your parents to think I have no manners.”

“There’s no need for you to do that.”

“But—”

“I promise. They think you’re fine,” she said hurriedly. Leaning a little bit closer, her smile turned brighter. “Caleb, have I told you that I think it’s so sweet of you to help me work on Christmas baskets?”

That was him, Mr. Sweet. Fact was, he would have helped her pick up snakes and spiders if that’s what she wanted. “You have,” he said, taking care to sound like he couldn’t care less. “Besides, you need some help going to everyone's houses to gather up all the donated items. It's a lot to carry."

"It is. So many people have offered to give so much. It's a wonder, don't you think?"

"Not so much. Everyone wants to help the needy this time of year."

"Oh. Yes, I suppose so." When she paused at the top of the steps, looking curiously deflated, Caleb reached out and held her elbow. Just to steady her. So she wouldn't trip or fall, of course.

When they reached the sidewalk he still had his hand cupped around her elbow. Actually, his hand had crept up and he was carefully holding her arm. When she looked into his eyes and blushed, he dropped his hand.

"Danke," she murmured. "The steps were a bit slick."

They paused, standing close together. Close enough for him to notice the little flecks of silver in her blue eyes. To see that there were five freckles, not six, that dusted her nose.

Close enough that if he leaned down just a little bit, he could brush his lips against her forehead. Or maybe even her cheek. Or maybe even . . .

Clearing his throat, he stepped back. "We better get going," he said. "It's too cold to just stand here."

"All right, Caleb," she said with a hint of a smile.

As they started walking—side by side but not touching—Caleb wondered how much longer he could go before he made a complete fool of himself and told her that he really liked her.

Before he leaned in and actually did kiss her.

Before he risked getting his heart stomped on while she laughed at him.

Hopefully none of that would happen until well past Christmas Day.

Chapter Two

Nine Days Until Christmas

"Judith? Are you ever going to answer me?" her mother asked from the other side of the kitchen.

Judith, practically up to her elbow in mashed potatoes, glanced at her mother's way. "I'm sorry?"

"I asked you if you had time to change the sheets on Maggie and Toby's beds. Did you?"

She hadn't. How had she forgotten? Feeling like she was in a daze, she replied, "*Nee*, Mamm. I'm sorry, I forgot to do that."

"That isn't like you. You never forget to do your chores." Tilting her head to the side, she looked at Judith through narrowed eyes. "Are you not feeling well?"

"I'm fine. I just forgot, that's all." Finally satisfied that the potatoes were good and mashed, Judith carried the bowl over to her mother. "Would you like me to put these on the table now, or warm them in the oven?"

"Judith, it's only five thirty. You know we don't eat until six o'clock. Put them in the oven."

Dutifully Judith did that. Then, fearing she was either about to be grilled more by her mother or given another dinner dish to prepare, she wiped her hands on her apron and scooted out of the kitchen. "I'll go change those sheets now."

"Now it is too late. You can do it after supper—"

"I'd rather get it over with," she interrupted. "I have a new book I'd like to read tonight."

"I see. Well, all right . . ."

Just as her mother took another breath, Judith escaped to her little brother and sister's room. The two youngest shared a room. Judith figured eventually Maggie would move into another room, but for now they seemed content to share.

It looked like they were determined to keep it messy as well. Looking around at the toys on the floor, the wooden puzzle pieces scattered around the area carpet, and their towels from the night before left on the ground, Judith sighed.

Her mother would expect her to locate her brother and sister and make them clean their room while she changed their sheets.

But if she did that, she would still not get a moment's peace. And she really needed that.

Decision made, she closed their door and got to work stripping the beds.

As the quiet sank into her soul, she finally breathed easier.

Because all she could seem to do was think about the man she'd seen the day before. Ben Knox.

Ben Knox!

What had it been about him that had struck her fancy, all over again? Well, other than his handsomeness, his confident attitude . . . and the way he looked at her, just like she was someone worth staring at?

Oh, for heaven's sakes! There was no question that the thing about Ben was that he'd always held her attention, for better or worse. Maybe it was his confidence. Maybe it was that smile of his? Whatever it was, there had always been something about him that made her want to be just a little bit bad.

Not really bad. Just a little bit.

No, he just made her want to forget about her responsibilities and imagine only thinking about herself. And her wants. Benjamin Knox made her wish she could go walking with him instead of doing chores.

Made her wish she could spend time by his side, just talking and laughing . . . instead of working at the store.

Made her want to be thankful for her clear complexion and pretty eyes, just for a little while—because he looked like he appreciated them. As she remembered the way his eyes examined her, she shivered. Again . . .

Of course, he had no idea she felt that way. No one did.

To the world, she was simply dutiful

Judith. The girl who always did what was expected of her. The girl who sometimes looked down on those who did not do the same.

Snapping a bottom sheet, she spread it across the twin bed. In no time, she had one bed finished and unfolded the next bottom sheet.

Just as the door opened.

"Whoever you are, get to picking up these toys," she ordered. "This is a mess."

"If I pick up three farm animals, will I get to talk with you for a while?"

Judith whirled around. There, standing in the doorway, was her sweet cousin-in-law Clara. Tim's wife. "I'm so sorry. I was sure you were either Maggie or Toby."

"I figured that." Crossing her arms over her expanding middle, Clara smiled. "When your mother told me you were up in their room making beds, I thought she was teasing. Don't you ever get a chance to sit?"

"Not lately." Looking over at her good friend, she asked, "What brings you here? Are you staying for dinner?"

"*Nee*. Tim wanted to talk to your father for a few minutes, and I wanted to see you. Do you have time to talk?"

"I do." As she smoothed the quilt back on top of Maggie's bed, she said, "I'll leave these sheets for them to take downstairs. Come into my room with me. How are you?"

After rubbing her tummy, she spread her arms wide, the motion pulling her black apron taut. "I'm as big as a house!"

Clara was six months along. "You're big, but not quite that big," Judith quipped. "Actually, I don't think you've ever looked more beautiful."

Looking Clara over more carefully, she noticed some new things. Clara's cheeks were flushed and her eyes were bright. In addition, she looked so happy that not even the ever-present scar on her cheek looked like it could dim her mood. "I mean, you really do look *wunderbaar*."

"Danke." The moment they were both in Judith's room, Clara closed the door and leaned back on it. "Guess what? We're going to have twins!"

Judith sat down on her pale pink quilt in a rush. "Truly?"

"You look befuddled. I felt the same way when we got the news," Clara said with a rush. "Tim and I just found out this afternoon. Actually, we've just left the doctor's office. She decided to give us an ultrasound because she was concerned about how much baby I had. It turns out I have two instead of one! I need to take it easy now."

"I should hope so."

"Tim is going to help finish up my school year, so he's downstairs letting your dad know he can't help with the store anymore."

"He can't?" She hated it, but a knot of panic formed in her stomach. If Tim couldn't help out, Caleb was at the brick factory, and Josh was busy helping Gretta get settled in their new home . . . how was she going to survive in the store until Christmas?

Clara—always the caretaker—patted her hand. "Don't worry. We already came up with a solution. Your father's going to hire some extra help."

"We've never done that before."

"There's a first time for everything, *jah*? This will be a good thing. Even though Josh agreed to help out as much as he can, Gretta's *doktah* told her not to pick up anything heavy, and that means baby Will."

"I guess it will be good for the family, but . . . I don't know who Daed could hire." Everyone who she might depend on to help out was already either working somewhere else or busy with their lives.

"You don't need to worry about that. It's all taken care of. Tim spoke with Joshua. They took your father over to meet a friend of Joshua's earlier this evening."

"And who would that be?"

"Benjamin Knox."

"Ben?"

Clara blinked. "*Jah*. Do you remember him, too?"

"We were in the same grade in school."

"That's right. I forgot." Curving her arms over her distended belly, Clara glanced out the window. "He's been gone so long, I keep forgetting that *of course* we all know each other."

"Well, we all kind of know him." Remembering how he'd rarely joined in at singings, how he'd often eaten his lunch by himself, she said, "You know how Ben always kept himself at a distance."

"Or we kept him there," Clara murmured, sounding a little sad. "Where it was safe." Glancing toward Judith, her wistful smile turned bright. "Ben always seemed just a little bit dangerous, don'tcha think?"

"Clara, I can't believe you're saying such things."

"I'm not saying anything wrong. Just the obvious." Clara shrugged. "Anyway, that's who Tim and your father talked to."

Jumping to her feet, Judith walked toward the door. "Clara, I should really go talk to my father about Ben. I mean, I'm going to be the one who has to work with him."

Clara lumbered to her side. "Judith, what's wrong? Tim and Josh thought you'd be so happy about the news. You need some help."

"I know."

"Then what is wrong?"

What wasn't? Marching down the stairs, Judith didn't know how to respond without hurting Clara's feelings. So she held her tongue. With effort.

But as she got to her father's side, everything that was on the tip of her tongue disappeared. Her *daed* looked relieved. Tim looked pleased. Joshua and Gretta were all smiles.

And that's when she knew she wasn't

going to be able to say a thing. It wouldn't be right to upset everyone.

She'd just have to deal with Ben and her mixed-up, twisted feelings toward him all by herself.

The house was quiet. Of course, it always had been. After heating up a can of soup, Ben sat at the table with a book he'd borrowed from the library and a battery-operated lamp.

Funny how this lonely dinner was still better than most of the meals he'd eaten here.

Tentatively, he blew on his spoon, then slurped down the first taste of Campbell's vegetable soup. The broth tasted good enough, the hot broth coating his throat and slowly warming up his insides.

Satisfied that his meal was the right temperature, he opened the novel to the first page, adjusted the lamp, and proceeded to read the same page three times.

Frustrated, he closed the novel and leaned back. Knowing he couldn't concentrate because he was thinking about the wariness he'd spied in Judith's eyes. And was remembering the conversation he'd had with her father and brother.

It seemed that it didn't really matter how long he'd been gone. Memories didn't fade, or maybe it was reputations that didn't.

Because, sure enough, most of the people he'd come in contact with were sure he was still eager to cause trouble.

What they didn't realize was his "trouble" had been greatly exaggerated. For the majority of his time in Sugarcreek, he'd spent just the way he was at the moment. Alone, with only the company of a book.

It was a bitter pill to swallow—knowing that he hadn't changed all that much over the years. *"Here you go, Ben,"* he told himself with more than a bit of irony lacing his voice. *"Here you are, sitting by yourself yet again. Another big night for you."*

Ever since he'd turned thirteen, he'd had an angry streak that he fostered, at least in reputation. That had been the year his mother had gone off to "visit" her parents. And had never quite made it back.

His father had sworn him to silence. So instead of telling people he no longer had a mother living at home, he'd been forced to say that she'd been "under the weather."

His father had retreated further into himself, except for bursts of anger directed at him and his sister, Beth. It turned out the only thing that helped Beth was for their father's anger to settle on him. Then his *daed* could yell at him to his heart's desire and leave her alone.

Which he did with startling regularity.

All three of them seemed to do all right with that arrangement, at least on the outside. Beth had stayed around after she finished eighth grade, cooking him meals and doing his laundry as best she could.

In return, he stayed in school another year and gave his father someone to direct his anger toward.

Out of desperation, Ben tried to take comfort in the knowledge that at least he was protecting his sister.

But soon he grew up. His famous short temper became shorter, and his sharp tongue became lethal. He became too big for their father to take out his frustration on. Before long, Beth left, too. The moment she turned eighteen, she left for Aunt Beth's—to live with the woman she'd been named after.

And after six months there, she had caught the eye of a boy, an *Englischer* named after Austin or Houston or some Texas city. And though she was young, and though she didn't know the *Englischer* with the city name all that well, she eloped with the kid.

Ben hadn't heard from her since.

He knew why. Beth had left Sugarcreek and moved on to show him that it was possible. In her own way, she'd hoped her actions would save him. In the letter she'd left for him, she'd encouraged him to get out of Sugarcreek, too. Too leave the church and get a driver's license. To start over. But all Beth's leaving had really done was make his world seem even darker and more isolated.

He didn't know why, but he'd never been in that much of a hurry to stop being Amish. He liked the way of life, even if his life wasn't all that great.

So he'd stayed and worked odd jobs and argued with his father. But after a while, all of that gave him no satisfaction, either. So he'd left, too.

Now, three years later, his father was long

gone. Ben had come back to take care of the house and put it up for sale.

He'd intended to only stay in Sugarcreek as long as that took.

But then he'd seen Judith and felt old feelings that he had forgotten even existed. Feelings about longing and hope and happiness. Her father and cousin Tim had surprised him when they asked if he wouldn't mind helping their family out for the two weeks before Christmas. It might make good sense, since his house was on the market anyway.

Ben hadn't been lying when he said he wouldn't mind helping out. Not one little bit. So for the next nine days he was going to get to be by Judith. Much of the time alone.

For hours at a time. Seeing her smile. Looking at her face. Talking with her.

For a few hours a day he was going to pretend that he, too, was filled with the joy of the season. That he understood that feeling of hope and expectation that seemed to be on everyone's mind. That he was anxiously awaiting Christmas Day.

All that would be lies, of course.

Because when he was sitting here at the table, sipping soup and reading, he knew the exact opposite would be true.

He was going to wish Christmas Day would never come.

Chapter Three

Nine Days Until Christmas

The minute she heard the front door open, Lilly jumped up from her laptop and hastily turned it off.

"Lilly? Lilly, where are ya?"

"I'm up here, Robert. I'll be right down."

But instead of waiting for her to meet him in the kitchen, Robert took the stairs two at a time and scooped her up off the top of the landing. When she squealed, he laughed, the sound deep and rich and wonderful.

"Have I managed to surprise you, wife?"

he asked as he twirled her around, making the skirt of her jade green dress billow out like an umbrella.

"Very much so." Resting her hands on his shoulders, she looked down at him. "Robert, put me down! You're going to hurt yourself."

"I'm not so old that I can't pick my *frau* up whenever I want," he said with a smile. But still, he gently set her down, letting her body glide against his as he did so, then wrapping his hands around her waist.

Making her feel so wanted and loved. Humbled. "Why are you home so early?"

"I closed up shop. Snow's coming, so Daniel gave me a ride home. That, and well, I couldn't wait to see you."

Before she could reply to that, he kissed her, making her remember just how much she had to be grateful for this Christmas. A little over a year ago she'd been so depressed she'd worried that she would never find her way out. She'd gone through the embarrassment of discovering she was pregnant from a high school ex-boyfriend, had suffered a miscarriage, and then had fallen head over heels in love with Robert Miller. On paper, he had seemed like her exact opposite. He was older, a widower, and was Amish.

Because he'd also known terrible heartache, they shared a connection neither could deny. From the moment he'd kissed her in the middle of a corn maze, they both realized they'd found their perfect match. However, things hadn't been easy. Lilly had felt that she couldn't become Amish for Robert . . . and he loved his faith so much she couldn't ask him to leave it. So she broke things off, loving him so much that she couldn't bear to make him give up his faith for her. But he'd loved her just as much—and left the order. Eventually, they compromised and joined a conservative Mennonite church.

Things for both of them changed drastically. Being Mennonite opened a whole new world to Robert. Phones and cars and electricity were available to him now. For Lilly, it had meant embracing a faith enough to give up jeans and makeup and short hair. While they couldn't say the transition had been easy, the fact that they were both willing to go through such hardships was bringing them closer together.

Now it was moments like this—when he

looked at her as if there was no other person in the world that he wanted to see—that made her feel giddy inside.

When Robert finally lifted his head, she smiled at him. "I'm very glad you came home early. Would you like some coffee or tea?"

"*Kaffi* would be most welcome."

"I'll brew you a fresh pot."

As he followed her down the stairs, then stretched out his legs while he watched her fill up the coffee maker, he said, "What have you been doing today?"

"You know I worked this morning."

"I know that, to be sure. Since you dropped me off at work."

Lilly felt her cheeks heat. He still wasn't all that eager to learn to drive, so she was the designated driver. Though he seemed fine with that, sometimes it made her uncomfortable. Not because she minded driving him—never that. But because it sometimes reminded her of just how different his life was now.

"What have you been doing since you got home?"

"Oh, this and that," she said airily. "Laundry and cleaning."

But instead of looking pleased, he eyed

her with concern. "I told you that you didn't need to worry about having a spotless house, Lilly. You are still working at the Sugarcreek Inn. I don't want you to wear yourself out."

"I'm not weak, Robert."

"I know that."

Her working had been a matter of contention between them. At first, Robert had wanted her to quit her job as a waitress and stay home—not because he minded her working, but he felt that she tried to do too much.

"Lilly, I hate to think of you never giving yourself time to rest or to see your friends, or even to play on your computer."

At the mention of her laptop, Lilly flushed. That was always how he phrased it—her *playing*. As the coffee continued to brew, she turned and leaned back against the kitchen counter. "As a matter of fact, I was upstairs sitting on the guest-bedroom bed playing on the computer," she admitted. Almost like she was in trouble.

Something flickered in his eyes, but he only nodded.

"Have I told you that you look pretty today?"

This time she didn't bother to hide her emotions. "Gretta helped me finish this dress," she said proudly. "She brought it to me at the inn this morning."

"How much of this dress did you sew?" he asked, amusement lacing his voice.

"The outside seams. And I cut out the pattern. Well, I tried to do a sleeve but Gretta had to redo it." Fingering the fabric again, she admitted, "As soon as she brought it to me, I ran to the back and changed clothes. Kay hardly knew what to think."

"I bet she wasn't as entertained as the customers were by your quick change." He laughed. "Lilly, I love how honest you are with me. You make me smile."

"Still?"

"After all these *months*?" he asked, exaggerating the last word. "*Jah,* even after all these months."

After bringing him a cup of coffee, black with no sugar, she sat down next to him. "You used to visit me at work, you know."

He paused. "And so I did. Well, perhaps I'll walk down next time you're waitressing and have a piece of pie for lunch."

The warmth that was always so present

between them bloomed anew. “I hope you will,” she murmured.

Reaching out, he brushed his thumb against her cheek, just to feel her, she supposed. Then, after another moment, he cleared his throat. “So, I talked to my family. Though my *daed* was civil enough, he doesn’t feel like it would be right for us to visit on Christmas Day. He feels it might be too awkward.”

“I’m sorry he feels that way.” With effort, she refrained from saying anything more. His family, especially his cousin, had seemed to go out of their way to make sure Robert knew that he wasn’t part of their family anymore. She’d naively imagined that they would come around after just a few weeks.

But of course that had just been a pipe dream. She worried that Robert’s cousin Abe had continued to make his displeasure evident. And she had a feeling that he was littering Robert’s parents’ minds with doubts.

Robert continued to look away, making her feel even more sorry for him.

“My father did say that we could see them on the twenty-sixth.”

Though she was tempted to say something sharp, like that was big of them, she knew sarcasm would only make him feel worse. Instead, she kept her voice even. "I will look forward to seeing them. Would they like to come over here?"

"No. They thought perhaps we could meet them at a restaurant. Or we could go to their home."

So they still didn't want to step foot in their house. Lilly supposed she shouldn't have been surprised. Technically, it was only Robert's—it was the house he'd built for Grace, his first wife who'd died much too young.

Though Robert had said time and again how glad he was that Lilly lived here now—that he was glad she was changing things here and there—Lilly knew his family didn't feel the same way.

In their minds, she had ruined Robert. For her, he'd left them, left their community. She'd made him different.

That wasn't true. Robert was still upstanding and serious and kind. He still believed in the Lord and tried to be a good Christian man. Only now he wore jeans.

And smiled. Well, he smiled when he wasn't dwelling on his family.

A small, petty part of her wanted to hurt them, too, but she loved Robert too much to play such games. "A restaurant is fine. Their home is fine, too," she added. "Wherever you want to see them is fine with me."

"Fine." His lips twitched. "Well, they're trying, I suppose."

When she noticed that his cup of coffee was already half gone, she grabbed the carafe and took it to the table. Her hand trembled as she carefully poured coffee into his favorite mug.

"You're not going to say much about my family, are you? Or how you feel about how they are treating you."

"I wouldn't dream of it."

His eyes sparkled. "I had no idea you could be so closemouthed."

"Me, neither. Actually, I'm more than a little proud of myself," she said with a smile. "You should be impressed."

"I am." After another sip, a shadow fell across his brow. "I've got something else to tell you."

"What is that?"

He took out his pocket watch. "It broke," he said.

Taking the chair next to him, she picked up the timepiece and examined it more closely. The glass face was shattered. The silver case surrounding the face looked a bit mangled, too. "Perhaps we could get it fixed?"

"I don't know. I'm thinking it's well and dead." He sighed as he took another sip of the hot brew. "It must have fallen out of my pocket today when I wasn't aware of it. I was working on sanding a hope chest when my boot got it well and good."

Reaching out, she clasped his hand. "I'm sorry, Robert. I know the watch was special to you."

"It was my grandfather's. But it was more special to me because I used it for the time," he said with a wry smile. "Now I'm going to be forced to walk to my office to know what time it is."

"We'll think of something," she said, suddenly having a very good idea about his Christmas present. Afraid if she didn't redirect the conversation he was going to talk about replacing it right away, she said, "Let's not worry about it for now."

"All right. Now that we won't be seeing my family, I was wondering how you would like to spend Christmas Day."

She'd been thinking about their plans for some time. "Since we're going to my parents' house on Christmas Eve, and services at our new church before that . . . how about we stay home, just the two of us?" she ventured. "I know it might be kind of quiet, but sometimes quiet is good."

His eyes widened. "You'd be okay with that? Just being here, together?"

"Of course, Robert." Speaking from her heart, she said, "I love being with you more than anyone else in the world. I think spending the day together, celebrating Jesus's birth here at home sounds like a really nice way to spend Christmas." Who knows? Maybe she'd even be able to make a turkey or a ham and not burn it.

Leaning close, he brushed his lips against hers once more. "I'd be happy with that, too," he murmured into her ear as he leaned closer.

As he rubbed her back, seeming to find comfort in just her presence, Lilly relaxed against him. When they hugged like this, when he spoke to her like she was everything to him, Lilly was sure that everything was right in the world. And felt more optimistic about their future together than ever before. "I'm glad you came home early," she murmured.

"Me, too." He pressed his lips to her temple, his now smooth-shaven cheek gliding smoothly against her skin before locating her mouth.

After a time, he whispered in her ear again. "If we're alone on Christmas, I'll get to see how much you enjoy my present for you. All by myself."

"What did you get me?"

"You know I won't tell. You're going to have to wait a little longer."

"But—"

He pressed a finger to her lips. "No more prying, Lilly. Besides, I haven't been pressing you for information, have I?" Before she could reply, he stepped back and looked at her very smugly. "Fair's fair. Right?"

"Right," she replied. Because, after all, what could she say? But inside, that same knot of worry that had threatened to strangle her got even bigger.

When he left the kitchen, she prayed

that she would one day become the woman he believed her to be.

Better.

She so wanted to make him proud of her. To have him be pleased with her. And right now, if he didn't like her gift, she was sure that he was going to be terribly disappointed.

Maybe even think about another woman who used to be in his life. The woman who'd been so special and perfect.

And he'd find Lilly wanting. Maybe even have regrets about his marriage.

She would just hate that. Could there be anything worse than for their first Christmas together to be filled with regrets and doubts?

With a lump in her throat, she knew there would be something far worse . . . that Robert's feelings would start to turn.

Chapter Four

Eight Days Until Christmas

This had been the longest three hours of her life.

"So do you have any more questions about checking packing slips and filing them away?" Judith asked Ben as she shuffled a few more papers around.

They were standing side by side behind the front counter, close enough that she could smell the scent of his soap on his skin. Close enough for her to notice that he had a small pair of scars on his jaw.

And for her to wonder just how he got them. And when.

Looking at her directly in the eye, Ben shook his head. “I don’t have a single question. Not one.”

His reply would have meant a whole lot more if he’d ever even looked at the papers. If he’d even acted interested with what she had to say. Instead, all he seemed inclined to do was grin and stare at her.

Which, of course, made her even more flustered.

And notice that his hazel eyes were really more blue than green. At least around the edges.

“Ben, this is serious.”

“Believe me. I will never take the invoices lightly. Ever.”

Those eyes of his were sparkling again. And his cheek—well, his cheek had the smallest of dimples on it. Just like he was completely amused by her. “Ben . . .”

He laughed under his breath before turning toward two new customers. “*Wilkum*!” he said with a smile. “How may I help you?”

The English tourists beamed as they

faced him in surprise. As Judith watched the women look him over, notice his broad shoulders and his perpetually tanned face, they looked like they'd just won the jackpot. "We were just looking around. For Christmas gifts. Do you have anything Christmasy here?"

Judith was just about to inform the ladies that her family's store was the wrong place to look for ornaments with Amish characters painted on them when Ben walked around the counter and directed the ladies to a collection of handmade baskets and cookbooks.

"These are made by people in the community. Perhaps they'd make perfect gifts for your friends and family?"

The younger woman looked starstruck. "Oh, yes, they would, indeed."

With a wink in Judith's direction, he said extremely courteously, "Please let me know if I can help ya further."

After the ladies simpered, Ben practically sauntered back Judith's way. But instead of returning to stand near her behind the counter, he stayed on the other side. Resting his elbows on the wood and looking completely satisfied. "How am I doing, Boss?"

His pride would have been shameful if she hadn't been so impressed. "Ben, I think they're buying a dozen cookbooks between them. And four baskets, too. It's amazing."

But instead of gloating, his expression turned solemn. "*Gut*. I'm glad you're happy with me."

He caught her off guard. What did he mean by that? Had she been so difficult to please?

Or . . . was he simply trying to get her gander up? Again? "I didn't mean to sound surprised . . ."

"But you are surprised, ain't so?"

Because he was still staring at her intently, she nodded. "Helping customers is good. Encouraging them to buy more than they intended is something that's difficult for me."

"Why?"

"I don't know. I guess I don't want to push things at them."

"But you're not forcing them to buy, just suggesting—"

"Like I said, you are far better at this than I am."

"I doubt that, Judith." His gaze had softened. His voice had lowered. He'd leaned a little closer and made her want to lean closer, too. Which, of course, made her pulse quicken.

Luckily the English ladies approached.

She cleared her throat while Ben backed up with a jerk. "Did you find everything you were looking for?"

"We did. Well, we did over in this section," the older of the pair said with a laugh. "Could we set these puzzles and candles on the counter?"

Judith nodded. "But of course."

"What else may I help you with?" Ben asked.

"Baked goods. Do you have any rolls?"

"We do. Made fresh this morning."

The *Englischer* smiled. "I want some of those. I'm so glad we came in today. I found everything I needed."

Judith checked out two other customers, greeted a newcomer, and then eyed Ben in amazement as he stacked one, two, three, four containers of rolls, one block of cheddar cheese, and three boxes of cinnamon rolls and cookies in her arms.

How did Ben do that? He was a true salesman, able to encourage customers to buy things that Judith could only dream about. She couldn't help but be slightly envious of his accomplishments—during the three days that Ben had worked, store sales had greatly risen.

Two hours later, when she was locking up after the last customer left, she felt obligated to give Ben the praise he deserved. "You're a *gut* worker, Ben Knox."

He looked at her for maybe a little longer than necessary, then shrugged. *"Danke."*

She felt embarrassed. It was faint praise for everything he'd did. Plus, even to her ears it sounded vaguely condescending. "I'm sorry. You are more than just a good worker. You sell real well—and you're good with the customers, too. You seem to be a natural fit. Everyone's noticed. My *daed* is real pleased."

"Is he?" He crossed his arms over his very broad chest. "And what about you?"

"What about me?" Now she was feeling

even more out of sorts. The way he looked at her made her imagine they were the only two people in the world.

"Are you pleased with me, Judith Graber?"

That deep tone of his sent a little shiver down her spine. "Yes. I mean, I just told you I thought you worked hard. That . . . that I thought you did a *gut* job . . ." For heaven's sakes. She didn't know what she was saying!

"And that is all?"

His tone wasn't harsh. It wasn't critical. No, instead it sounded . . . sad? Disappointed?

No matter how it sounded, it made her feel tongue-tied. "Ben, I don't know what you want me to say . . ."

His face went blank as he stepped away, breaking the connection she wasn't even sure they'd had. "Of course you don't. Forgive me. I shouldn't have pressed you like that. Is there anything else you'd like me to do?"

Shouldn't have pressed her? "*Nee.* You can go."

"What about you?"

Pasting a smile on her face that she didn't feel, she shrugged. "I won't be leaving for a while now. I have to finish the deposit before I go home."

He scowled. "But it's dark out."

"I know."

"Then you'll hitch up your horse and drive home?" When she nodded, wondering why he looked so perturbed, a hard expression entered his eyes. "I'll wait for you."

"There's no need—"

"There's every need," he interrupted. "I don't want you here alone at night."

He didn't want her to be alone at night? "Ben, it is no problem. It is certainly not your problem, anyway."

For a moment, it looked like he was going to refute that. "Judith, I'll wait here with you."

He was making her *naerfich*. Nervous and confused. "But I do this all the time. By myself."

"You won't while I'm here." He lowered his voice. "If I could, I'd make sure you never were here alone. And I'd certainly drive you home in your buggy."

He was truly making her feel flustered now. The way he was looking at her, the way he was talking to her . . . well, no one had ever spoken to her like that before.

Like she was special. Needed to be protected.

Half afraid she was going to accept, Judith strived to keep her voice matter-of-fact. Professional. "Well, now, Ben. That is mighty kind of you, but I'm sure you have other things to do. Or, you know, other people to see."

For a moment, she didn't think he was going to answer her. It truly looked like he was afraid to. Then he sighed. "Judith, I promise you this. There's nothing else for me to do and no one waiting for me. Let me stay with you. Staying ain't a big thing."

There was something in his voice that sounded too familiar. She knew that desperation, even if she wasn't all that sure what his reasonings behind it were.

"All right, then, Ben. If you wouldn't mind waiting, I'd be most grateful."

"I don't mind waiting at all. It would be a pleasure."

The look of satisfaction in his eyes made her heart beat a little faster.

Chapter Five

He was going down a slippery slope at lightning speed, and that was a fact. As Ben sat on a worn stool and pretended he didn't mind fiddling with a basket of red and gold jingle bells while Judith Graber worked, his mind spun.

All his life, he'd been pushed to the side. His parents had had their own troubles and to them he'd been a constant reminder of past mistakes.

In short, he'd never felt wanted and had compensated for that by attempting to be tougher and harder than most other people.

He'd developed an attitude that was just arrogant enough to push people away.

And it had served him well. His hard exterior forced most people to give him a wide berth. To keep him at a distance.

Unable to sit still any longer, he got to his feet and walked down the store's aisles. Straightening stock was a mindless job, but far better than doing nothing.

In school, as the years passed and his home life became unbearable, he'd felt so fragile inside he developed an even harder shell.

He concentrated on keeping his heart safe instead of making friends. He worried about his future instead of his studies. He developed a talent for putting other people down and for never turning away from a fight. And along the way, he earned himself quite a reputation.

Most kids shied away from him. After a time, their teacher practically washed her hands of him, too.

His parents had gone from not wanting him to not expecting much. Then, of course, his *mamm* left and his *daed* spiraled down into a terrible depression. Before long, his sister left. And there was no way his shell was going to break.

Remembering how quiet his house had become, Ben grasped a sack of flour too hard. A puff of flour burst into the air as it gave way. Picking up the ruined sack, he walked to the bulk food area to deposit the contents in the flour bin.

Judith glanced up as he passed. "Everything all right?"

"Jah." He lifted the damaged sack so she could see. "This opened. I'm going to go take care of it."

"Danke." She smiled in a distracted way before going back to adding receipts.

Ben darted down another aisle. Out of Judith's sight.

Which didn't matter of course.

There was only one person who he'd wished had been able to see through his tough attitude: Judith Graber. How, he didn't know. As a little girl, she'd been looked after by her older brother, Josh. As she'd gotten older, she'd been surrounded by Caleb and all her friends.

And all her admirers.

He wasn't surprised. Judith was the type

of girl to sit with kids who were awkward and alone. She helped others with their homework. She even smiled at boys everyone else avoided. *Jah,* she was a lovely person, both inside and out.

But he had felt a dark hole inside of himself whenever they spoke. Because while she had been everything good to him, it had always been obvious that she was only being near him out of a misplaced sense of duty. That if she'd had her way, she would probably do just about anything to never see him again.

Now wasn't any different.

Truly, it was taking virtually everything he had to be closed off and arrogant with Judith. To him, she was perfection. Not in a polished, too-shiny kind of way, like the fancy *Englischers* in the gift shops.

No, her perfection was that she wasn't perfect. She worked hard and was almost abrupt with others. But she also had a yearning look in her eyes that told him she wished for far more in her life than merely a job well done. That longing, of course, made her all the more desirable to him. He was too flawed to fancy someone who had none.

And all that wasn't even taking into consideration her looks. Which were lovely indeed. Thinking about the fine lines of her jaw, about the intelligence in her eyes, he knew that though he had changed some, his interest in her never had.

Once again, he ached for a place in her life.

Flour now disposed of, he walked back by the front counter.

When he approached, she placed her pencil in a drawer and carefully set the ledger on the center of the counter. "I'm ready to go now," she said.

He practically clapped his hands in relief. "All right, then. Let's get you on your way before it gets any later. Where's your cloak?"

"Ben, why are you fussing so?"

"I don't know," he lied. "Do you have a cloak?"

"But of course. It's in the back. Follow me."

They walked through the quiet aisles, their footsteps echoing along the finely hewed wood floors. If things were different between them, he would have reached for her hand.

Yeah, right. Who was he kidding? If things had been different between them, he would have wrapped an arm around her slim shoulders and held her close. Just to make sure she didn't get chilled.

In the small cloakroom, he spied her cloak. Before he knew what he was doing, he plucked it off the brass hook and carefully covered her shoulders.

When she lifted her hands to tie the strings, their fingers brushed. As if she was shocked, she tensed, then tied a bow. He put his wool coat on while she slipped her black bonnet on her head and secured that, too.

Unwilling to leave her side, he held open the back door for her and then waited while she locked up.

"I feel bad, making you stay with me," she said as they walked to the covered stalls and began hitching up Beauty.

"Don't." He rubbed the mare's flank as he made sure all the fastenings were secure. When they guided the horse outside and the cold blast of wind and snow pelted their skin, he held the horse steady while she climbed into the buggy.

"I'll close the barn door for you. Be safe,

now," he said, trying not to let on how pretty he thought she was, with her skin glowing from the light reflecting off the lantern and the pristine snow.

"I will." She gave a little wave, then motioned the horse forward.

As the horse clip-clopped away, he dutifully shut the barn door. Then, with nothing else to do, started for home.

Stomping his boots a bit to warm his feet, Ben tried to recall what he had at home to eat. Maybe some peanut butter? Crackers . . .

"Ben?"

He stopped and stared at Judith. She'd stopped her buggy on the side of the road and was looking at him with concern.

He raced forward. "Is something wrong?"

She bit her lip. "*Nee.* It's just, well . . . I was just thinking that perhaps you'd like to come home with me."

If she'd started dancing in the streets and singing at the top of her lungs, he couldn't have been more surprised. Like the fool that he was, he gaped.

Then he got his bearings. She needed help. That's what she needed. Of course.

"I'd be happy to drive you home. I wasn't lying about that."

"It's not that. I just started thinking, you don't have anyone, do you?" Her eyes widened. "I mean, at home."

He didn't but that wasn't anything new. "I'm fine."

"I just was thinking, well, my *mamm* always makes plenty of food. And it's so terribly cold and snowy out. Perhaps you'd like a hot meal?"

That was it. She felt sorry for him. Pitied him.

The right thing to do would be to brush off her offer, because who wanted to be pitied?

But if he said no, he knew one thing absolutely—he wouldn't see her again until tomorrow.

And right at that moment, it felt like far too long.

Swallowing his dignity he climbed into the buggy and took over the reins. "I never pass up a hot meal," he said. Adding just enough cockiness that he hoped his pride wasn't completely flattened.

And with that, he snapped the reins and moved Beauty forward onto the near-empty road. Pretending all the while that he didn't notice how right Judith's body felt next to his.

That he didn't notice that she smelled lovely, like roses.

That he didn't all at once feel like the luckiest man in Sugarcreek.

Chapter Six

Eight Days Until Christmas

"Caleb, if I get stuck on your couch, help me up, wouldja?" Rebecca called out from underneath a pile of pillows and quilts.

From his chair to her right, Caleb craned his neck to try to see Becca, but even that little movement caused his muscles to scream out in pain. For the last three days, they'd collected cans, sorted them into two dozen baskets, picked up frozen chickens from a nearby poultry farm, then put those in one of his family's freezers at their store. It had been a lot of work, especially since he was sore from loading bricks into the kiln at the factory.

"Nope, if you get stuck, you're on your own. I don't think I'm going to be able to move anytime soon."

Maybe one of your siblings could run over to my house and tell my *mamm* that I won't be home soon. Maybe not for a few days. Do you think Anson would mind?"

Caleb couldn't help but smile as he contemplated the idea of being around Rebecca nonstop for days at a time. "*Nee.* I'm sure Anson wouldn't mind doing that chore at all. Especially since he's always looking into my business."

She chuckled as she shifted with a groan and finally sat up. "My little sister Amanda used to be the same way when she was younger. A nuisance, that's what she was."

"I'm sure she was nothing like Anson and his buddy Ty. They are both incorrigible."

As if he'd heard his name, Anson came in the room. As he looked from Caleb to Rebecca to Caleb again, his eyes narrowed. "Whatcha doing?"

"Recovering," Caleb said.

Anson took that as a reason to come closer. "From what?"

"We've been working on the Christmas baskets for the last three days," Rebecca said. "All we've been doing is gathering items and sorting them out. They are heavy."

"Really heavy," Caleb added. "We've also been wrapping gifts."

"I didn't know you knew how to wrap presents, Caleb," Anson said.

"I do now." Fact was, if he never saw another roll of bright red wrapping paper, it would be too soon. "I'm so tired I could sleep until Christmas Day."

"You better not!" Rebecca said with a laugh. "We still have to finish the baskets. And deliver them all."

"I could help," Anson said. "When are you two working on them again?"

"Tomorrow," Rebecca said before Caleb could let Anson know that his help was definitely not needed.

Anson positively beamed. "I'll let Mamm know I'm going to go with you," he said before turning away in a rush.

"See what I mean?" Caleb asked as he pushed himself off his chair and walked toward her. "He's a pest."

"He's cute. Of course, he's not as cute as his older brother." Holding her hands out, her eyes shone. "Help me up, wouldja?"

"Sure." Crossing to her, he bent slightly and grasped her hands. A careful yank pulled her up.

And then, there she was, standing right in front of him. Close enough that the hem of her dress tangled around his legs. Close enough for him to smell that faint hint of vanilla that always seemed to play upon her skin.

Close enough to make him dare to flirt a bit. "When you talked about a cute older *bruder* . . . were you speaking of Joshua?" he asked.

To his pleasure, Rebecca didn't step backward. Didn't pull away her hands. No, instead of looking frightened or uncomfortable, she shook her head. "I am not speaking of Joshua."

"Are ya speaking of me?"

Her dimples popped. "Perhaps."

Before he could stop himself, he blurted, "I think you're pretty, Rebecca. Mighty pretty."

"You do?"

He nodded. Then, fool that he was, he kept talking. "I like you a lot."

"I like you, too," she murmured.

Maybe this was the moment. Maybe right now, right here, he could put his hands around her and pull her even closer—

Becca stepped backward and let go of his hands and Caleb immediately felt her absence. The last thing he wanted was to scare her off, so he stepped backward, too. "Tomorrow, where would you like to meet?"

"How about here? Your mother told me she'd help me make some dishcloths for the baskets."

"I can meet you here after work. You know, you're sure doing a lot for these baskets. Why?"

Her expression shuttered. "Oh, I don't know. It's just nice to do something for other people, you know."

"I hope everyone will appreciate it." He frowned, privately wondering if any of the recipients will even think twice about how much work had gone into the gifts.

"I like putting the baskets together. It makes me happy."

"Of course it does. You're the most caring girl I've ever met, Rebecca. You're always thinking about other people." Unable to stop himself, he brushed two fingers against her cheek. Pushing back two strands of hair.

Enjoying the feel of her soft skin.

For a moment, her eyes fluttered shut. Just as if she was truly enjoying his touch.

But when her eyes opened and focused on his, there was a new wariness there. As if his praise didn't seem to go over very well. Instead of looking pleased, she looked embarrassed. "I'm sorry if I'm embarrassing you," he said. "I just wanted you to know how I felt."

"You didn't embarrass me. I better go now, though."

He didn't want to leave her side. And he hated the idea of her being outside in the dark and cold alone. "How about I walk you home? It's dark out."

"*Nee* . . . there's no need for that. I've got my bicycle."

"But it's still awfully dark. Judith has the buggy, but the courtin' one is here. I'll be happy to take you home in that. I'd like to."

For a moment, he thought she'd give in. But then she shook her head. "I'll just see you here tomorrow."

"But Rebecca, I don't feel right about you being alone—"

"I'll be fine. Truly," she said, iron in her voice.

When she walked to the front door, Caleb raced to her side. Something was wrong and he wasn't quite sure what it was. But he ached to make her happy.

"Hey . . . Rebecca?"

She stopped. "Yes, Caleb?"

He felt like an idiot, but he couldn't stop himself. "If I, um, kissed you on the cheek would you get mad?"

All at once the sparkle that he loved appeared back in her eyes. Right before she tucked her chin down. "*Nee.* I wouldn't get mad, Caleb."

Not needing another invitation, he curved his palms around her shoulders and leaned close. Tried real hard to ignore that her skin smelled fresh and clean and girlish.

"Raise your head, would you, Rebecca?" Eyes wide, she did just that. And then he pressed his lips on her velvety soft cheek.

It lasted all of two seconds. The blush that appeared right after made him think of roses under warm summer skies.

Moments later, her bonnet and cape on, he watched as she walked down his front walkway.

And Caleb was left standing there grinning.

"What are you lookin' at?" Anson asked when he came back out of the kitchen.

"Nothing."

"Had to be something. Hey, I talked to Mamm and she said I could go with you and Rebecca tomorrow."

The last thing Caleb wanted was an Anson chaperone. "You better not," he warned.

"But you said—"

"Anson, I don't want you around when I'm with Rebecca."

"She wants me there." Looking as ornery as ever, Anson turned away. "I'm going to go tell Mamm."

Caleb folded his hands across his chest as Anson ran off to do what he did best—get into someone else's business.

But instead of running to his mother to explain his side of the story, he leaned against the windowpane next to the front door and looked for a hint of Rebecca.

Already he couldn't wait to see her again. By just being herself, Rebecca had given him a sense of peace he hadn't felt in a very long time. For too long, he'd felt suspended between two worlds—the Amish one he'd been born into and the English one that surrounded them all.

Just a year ago, he'd been ready to cross the line and move away from Sugarcreek. His neighbor Lilly Allen had even taken him to her friends in Cleveland in case he wanted to stay with them for a spell.

But then he'd finally had a true conversation with his father and he realized he had choices. He could work at the brick factory instead of at the store or on their farm. And the pressure he'd felt to become the person everyone expected him to be had morphed into the freedom to become the person he wanted to be.

Thinking back, Caleb still couldn't believe what a revelation that had been. Receiving choices had been all he'd needed to make some for himself. Those choices had included Rebecca. He wanted her in his life. He needed her.

All he had to do was figure out how to get her to feel the same way about him.

* * *

"You drive a horse real good," Judith told Ben when he turned the buggy easily onto her house's long driveway.

He glanced at her in amusement. "Sometimes you say the strangest things. Didn't you think I'd be able to handle your buggy?"

"Well, yes . . ." She shook her head. "I'm sorry. I guess I was just looking for something to say." Obviously she wasn't terribly creative.

"*Nee.* It's my fault. I blurt out things a lot of the time. Sometimes I forget that every comment isn't a criticism." He halted Beauty then and pulled up the brake. "Is this a good place to stop? Or would you rather me guide her into the barn?"

"*Nee.* This is fine."

As she started to scramble out of the buggy, Ben stayed her with a hand. "Hold up. I'll help you out."

Just as she was about to tell him that she'd been getting in and out of buggies just fine without his help, he'd jumped down, walked around, reached for her hand with his one hand and her waist with his other and, before she could prepare herself, was swung out of the conveyance.

For one brief moment, she felt herself completely in his grip. He held her confidently, and with such a sure expression that she intuitively knew that was how he did all things.

Feeling her insides melting, Judith stepped away and cleared her throat. From somewhere, she needed to locate her backbone. After that, she needed to remember just how irritating he could be.

It probably wouldn't hurt to remember that he wasn't a man who stuck around, either.

He was most definitely not the type of man to dream about having a future with.

But as she stood there, mere feet from him, Judith started wondering why she didn't really believe that anymore.

"Judith?" Ben swallowed. "Are you all right?"

No. She was confused and feeling particularly vulnerable. She was just attempting to figure out how to tell him that when her father came out of the barn.

"Benjamin, what a nice surprise. *Wilkum*."

Beside her, Ben stiffened. *"Danke."*

Even though she'd just firmly told herself

that . . . *I—am—not—attracted—to—Ben—Knox,* Judith found herself edging closer to him. Offering him security. "Ben offered to see me home, Daed. I invited him for dinner, too."

A bit of interest flickered in her father's expression before he nodded. "That's a fine idea. Why don't you two run on into the house? I'll take care of Beauty for you."

"I'm happy to do that for you, Mr. Graber," Ben said.

An almost-sympathetic look crossed her father's face before he smiled easily. "I know you would, Ben," her father replied. "And to be sure, you may take care of things another time. Now, though, why don't you walk Judith in? It's chilly out here."

Ben nodded and looked to Judith. "You ready to go inside?"

She loved how he did that—here he was giving her choices, not just following her father's directives blindly.

"I'm ready. Let's go and tell Mamm that we'll need to set one more place for dinner."

As they started walking, he looked her way again. "I hope she won't mind."

Well, that comment certainly lightened

her mood. “Ben. Have you not seen our family? Believe me, one more person won’t make a difference. Our mealtimes are chaotic and loud. No one will hardly notice you’re there.”

Chapter Seven

As Ben plopped a spoonful of mashed potatoes on his plate, then reached for the wiggling serving dish of carrots and peas from Judith's tiny sister Maggie, he was starting to think that Judith's comment hadn't been far off the mark. A Graber family dinner was chaotic, indeed.

As he looked around the wide wooden table, it was obvious that nearly every spot was filled. He wasn't the only guest. In addition to Mr. and Mrs. Graber, Judith, Caleb, Anson, Toby, and Maggie, there were at least five others. Ty Allen, who turned out to be Anson's best friend. Next to him were Tim Graber and his wife, Clara. Finally, to his great surprise, there were Mr. and Mrs. Allen, Ty's parents. And on the floor near Mrs. Allen sat their baby, Carrie, in a carrier.

No one seemed to care that the Allens were *Englischers*.

And no one had seemed too concerned that he was there, neither. In fact, the only person who gave him much attention was Judith. Which should have made him feel better but instead just set him on edge. Spending the day working at her side had made his infatuation complete. Now he had to be sure he didn't stare at her too often.

Even a smile from her could make him feel like stuttering.

"Ben?" Mrs. Graber prompted. "Would you mind quickly grabbing that platter of chicken from Maggie?"

With a start, Ben lifted the dish from the five-year-old's small, chubby hands. "Sorry," he muttered to her.

A shy one, Maggie turned away and simply reached for another plate.

"You've outdone yourself tonight, Irene," Mrs. Allen said. "Roast chicken, potatoes, peas and carrots, cornbread, and cranberry salad! It's a feast."

"You brought the chocolate-peppermint cake and the cranberry Jello-O and pear salad. Don't forget that, Barb."

As food continued to get passed and compliments abounded, Ben tried to remember if he'd ever had such a big meal. If he'd ever been a part of such a joyous, happy group.

He didn't know who he was trying to kid. Of course he hadn't. Dinners at his house—when there had been dinner—had involved silence and the barest of meals. They hadn't had much money for a bountiful table.

When everyone had finally been served, Mr. Graber said, "Let us give thanks for all our blessings."

As silence filled the air, Ben bowed his head and closed his eyes and prayed. Of course, there wasn't enough time for him to count all his recent blessings. He'd have to visit with the Lord late that night when he had all the time in the world.

But still, he thanked the Lord for the meal and the hands that made it, and of course, for the Grabers. When he lifted his head, he felt Judith's gaze on him.

"What?" he asked.

She shook her head. "Nothing. Please enjoy the meal."

He would've been more self-conscious if he'd felt that more of the people were paying attention to him. But in truth, no one really was. Clara and Tim were speaking with Mr. and Mrs. Graber about Christmas preparations, while Mrs. Allen was laughing with Ty and Anson about a sled crash they'd recently had.

Toby was showing Caleb a cut on his finger, and Judith was carefully cutting her chicken.

"You like?"

To his surprise, it seemed little Maggie was the only person interested in him. "Do I like what?"

She pointed to her pile of peas and carrots. "These." She wrinkled her nose in distaste.

Making him laugh. "*Jah.* You don't?"

After covertly glancing her mother's way, she shook her head. "*Nee,*" she whispered. Like she was sharing the most daring of secrets.

Feeling slightly silly, he said the thing he was supposed to say. Well, what he thought he was supposed to say, anyway. "You should like them. Vegetables make you stronger."

"Like you?" She pointed to his arm—to his bicep—with wide eyes. "You're mighty big."

To his astonishment, he found his cheeks turning hot. How sad was that? He was that unused to even the smallest of praise. "*Jah,* like me."

"You're gonna have to lift a mountain of peas to look like Ben," Anson said. "His arms are huge. Way bigger than Caleb's."

Caleb glared at his little brother. "Ben's older. Of course his arms are gonna be bigger."

Ty Allen joined in. "Do you lift weights?"

One by one, all the occupants looked at him. Right on cue, he felt his cheeks heat. "No," he said. "When I was with my aunt, I, uh, farmed a lot. It was hard work."

To Ben's relief, Tim leaned close to his wife and flexed his arm playfully. "See, Clara? You chose well. Us farmers are a hardy lot."

"You're going to need those muscles to carry around twins," Mr. Graber quipped.

"Clara thinks I'll do. Right, wife?"

Laughter erupted around the table as Clara teased him right back. Now that the focus was off him again, Ben leaned back in his chair.

Maybe he should have never agreed to take Judith home. He was poor company, that was for sure. Of course, if he hadn't, he wouldn't have been able to see she got home safe . . . or to enjoy the delicious meal.

"You're doing good," Judith said, leaning his way. "Please don't worry."

Embarrassed, he was about to tell her that he was definitely not worried. That he didn't need her support . . . but when he looked into her eyes, he knew he wasn't going to be able to say a thing.

Her eyelashes looked longer than ever, and they framed the most compassionate pair of blue eyes he'd ever had the good fortune to gaze into. When she blinked, his mouth went dry.

So all he did was jerk his head into a clumsy nod. And concentrate on his meal.

"When supper's over, do you want to play

with my animals?" Maggie asked. "I have a new goat."

"You have a what?"

After a furtive glance right and left, she pulled out a plastic white goat from under her apron. "See?"

"I'd love to," he said, knowing that little Maggie was surely wrapping his heart around her finger with every smile. "As long as I get to be in charge of the pig."

As he hoped, Maggie giggled. "Okay."

He was still smiling when he spooned up another amount of peas and carrots . . . and Maggie copied him.

And he knew he'd never felt so good as when Judith lightly squeezed his forearm at the end of the meal. Letting him know that everything was good—that he'd fit in just fine.

Of course, he knew things were much better than that.

Chapter Eight

"So, Ben Knox seemed to like supper," Caleb said to Judith as they waited outside in the hall for Maggie to finish in the bathroom.

Judith fought to control the vast array of emotions she was feeling. Though he hadn't said as much, she knew Ben had *loved* supper, and not just because of the food.

He'd noticed the red candles on a counter in the kitchen, and the bowl in the living room that was filled to overflowing with Christmas cards. He'd ran a finger along a red-and-green star quilt she'd made years ago, and smiled when Mrs. Allen had given her mother a glass bowl filled with pinecones.

In addition he'd seemed to absorb the comfort of her family as if he'd been thirsty for days. "He truly liked Maggie."

As she'd half expected, Caleb's gaze turned warm. "Who wouldn't?"

She really was the sweetest of all of them. Gentle and eager to please, their Maggie was the one member of the family who no one ever complained about. "Did you see him playing farm animals with her?" Judith shook her head. "I actually heard him squeal like a pig!"

"Maggie says he's her new best friend." Looking contemplative, he said, "So . . . what do you think of him?"

"Of Ben? Why, I don't know."

"He seems different than how I remember him."

"I think so, too. He smiles more."

"He smiles at you," Caleb corrected. "So, what do you think of him?" he asked again. When she paused, he clicked his tongue. "Come on, you have to think something. He's obviously half in love with you."

Judith turned to her brother in shock. "He

is not. We're just friends . . ." Though, had they actually ever been friends? "Plus he was excited for a home-cooked meal. He's on his own now, you know."

"I heard Mamm tell Daed that she wants Ben to take you home as often as possible now. I think she wants to feed him!"

"He'd love that."

"And maybe you would, too?"

Feeling awkward, she glared at him. "Why all the questions about me? I would've thought you wouldn't have any thoughts except for Rebecca."

"Oh, I think about Rebecca all the time." He shrugged, not looking the slightest embarrassed about his feelings. "I can't help it. It's just . . . the way you are with Ben—I've never seen you look smitten before."

She could understand that. After all, she'd never felt like this before. When she'd walked him outside, feeling so relieved that her father had made Ben borrow his bicycle so he wouldn't have to walk home . . . she'd been tempted to hug him good-bye.

Anything to keep him nearby for just a little bit longer.

"It's really too bad he's not planning to

stay here after Christmas," Caleb said, just as he knocked on the bathroom door. "Maggie? Did you get lost in there? Hurry up."

Judith was still thinking about Ben leaving when Maggie threw open the door and scampered down the hall.

Caleb paused. "Do you want to go first?"

"Nah, I don't mind waiting. You go ahead."

When Caleb closed the door and she was alone, Judith let herself think about Ben again. And imagine there really was something more between them.

Privately, she thought that was a terribly *gut* Christmas wish.

Seven Days Until Christmas

"Lilly, I'm amazed at how domesticated you've become," her mother said as she shopped beside her at the Walnut Creek Cheese Shop. "Never would I have guessed you would be spending your days planning dinner menus and cleaning house."

"Those things need to be done."

"Believe me, I know. It's just that you seem to being enjoying these chores. That's what's surprising."

Somewhere in there was a compliment.

Lilly was sure of it. But she felt a little embarrassed, too. Had her mother thought she was really so shallow? "You make me sound like I used to be a princess."

"Not at all. It's just you were always more of the type of girl to go to the mall and the movies instead of finding happiness baking cranberry bread." She paused. "Or washing towels and sheets."

"People change. I mean, look at Charlie." Her older brother had somehow turned into a dedicated student at college. The last time he'd come home, he told their parents that he'd been looking into scholarship opportunities so he could apply to law school. This was night and day from the way he'd been in high school, when everything was about him—and what he thought he deserved.

"Your brother's transformation has been impressive." Her mother smiled as she tucked a blanket more securely around Carrie. "People do grow up, it's true. Here Charlie is planning a career, you're married, and I've got a new little girl to look after! Who knows what Ty will have in store for us."

"If Anson's involved, it will be nothing good."

"Oh, those boys are growing and changing, too. As God intends for us all." Shaking her head in dismay, she said, "I never would have imagined I'd have another baby. But now I can't imagine life without Carrie."

"She is precious," Lilly agreed, almost able to completely stifle the pain that boiled up as she recalled her miscarriage just a year ago. If she'd had the babe, she probably never would have married Robert. She knew deep down that God had a plan for her. But as she watched her baby sister, it was hard to not think about that loss.

As they walked along through the grocery store, they stopped and looked at the fresh produce and headed toward the meats. Then she couldn't hold back her worries any longer. "Mom, I've got an idea about what to buy Robert, but I'm afraid he won't like it."

"That man is smitten with you. He will love anything you get him."

"I think he'd rather I made him something." Lilly bit her lip. Trying not to be so fixated on it, but unable to help herself.

"What is he getting you? Do you know?"

"He told me that he's making me something at his shop."

"That's sweet of him. He's a good man." She paused as she held up a package of bacon. "I shouldn't buy this, but I've been longing for bacon and eggs."

When her mother started talking about a recipe she found for a breakfast casserole, Lilly found her mind drifting.

Back to Robert. He really was a good man. A wonderful man.

Maybe that was the problem, she thought to herself. Here Robert had not only given up everything for her, but he knew exactly what to do to make her happy. She had no clue how to match that.

Directing the conversation back to Christmas, Lilly said, "Mom, I think I'm going to give him a new watch. One for his wrist, you know?" she clarified when her mom looked confused. "It will be expensive, but he's sure to really like a new watch, don't you think?"

"Well—"

"Or do you think it will send the wrong message?" Lilly quickly asked. "I don't want him to think he must adopt all English ways. But does a watch do that? I don't know."

"Lilly, Christmas is about celebrating Jesus's birth and about celebrating the love we have for each other. The gifts don't mean all that much . . . and you know the Amish don't value fancy gifts."

"But I want this Christmas to be really special."

"Lilly, it will be! Robert loves you. Anything you give him will be perfect. I'm sure he won't mind a store-bought gift. After all, he knew you couldn't cook or sew when he married you."

But Lilly was still worried about not being good enough "Mom . . ." she fretted, "maybe he hoped I'd become one?"

Her mother shook her head. "He hoped you'd love him. That's what he wanted from you, dear."

Lilly stifled a sigh. "He knows I love him. But that's not the point."

"Gifts aren't the point of Christmas, either, dear."

"I still want to give him something special." She bit her lip as she watched her mother put two packages of breakfast sausage in the cart, followed by a chicken. "Maybe I should get him a puppy?"

"I don't know if Midnight will care for that."

Thinking about her sleek black cat, who Robert had bought for her on their first real date, she nodded. "Midnight would either hide under the couch or hiss at the puppy."

"I'd stay away from pets."

"What did you and dad used to give each other when you first got married?"

A dreamy expression filled her mom's face, making her look even younger than usual. "All kinds of things. Candy. Clothes. One year your father gave me mixing bowls and spoons."

Mixing bowls and spoons sounded like horrible presents. "What was Dad thinking?"

Her mother laughed. "It was pretty romantic, if you want to know the truth. I used to make him cookies every Friday afternoon. He gave me the bowl so I'd never stop."

Lilly was flabbergasted. Who knew her father had a romantic streak? Who knew that her mother had been baking sugar cookies all this time for their father? "Wow."

As they walked toward to the front of the store, her mother tossed a loaf of bread in the cart, and finally picked up a poinsettia. "Don't worry, Lilly. You and Robert will begin your own traditions. And you'll know that whatever you decide to make or buy for him will the perfect thing."

"I hope so."

"I know so," her mother corrected as she pushed the cart to the open lane. "Now, let's get out of here before Carrie wakes up. She's been asleep for twenty minutes. We know our time is short."

Lilly laughed, then felt someone's gaze on her from across the way.

And saw Robert's cousin Abe and his wife, Mary. Both were staring at her, their gazes cool.

She stopped and looked at them, half hoping they would forget their anger about Robert marrying her and walk over and greet her kindly.

But instead of looking like they were going to forgive her anytime soon, Abe merely pulled out his watch, glanced at the time, then turned his back to her.

Making sure she had no doubt as to how they felt about her, and perhaps always would.

Chapter Nine

Seven Days Until Christmas

It wasn't the Amish way to put up Christmas decorations. Or a tree. Or sparkling lights. Not even a nativity.

Ben was fine with that. He'd never needed the English extravaganza that seemed to follow their need to celebrate a holiday until it was fairly beaten down and became tiresome.

But he couldn't get over just how quiet and depressing his home was.

Looking around, smelling the dust and the disuse and the memories— He shook his head. No, this didn't seem like a home at all. Just a house.

Here it was too quiet and too drab; there was no happiness. Once again, he was glad it was on the market and had already had a few showings. The day he found out it was sold would be a good one, for sure.

As he walked through the halls, trying to think of something to do until it was time to go to the Graber's store, Ben couldn't help but reflect on how different his house felt from the Graber family's home.

On his way home the night before, he kept thinking about what a happy place Judith had come from. He'd been reluctant to leave. Not just because he'd been next to Judith, but because he'd been surrounded by happiness.

Happiness was certainly something that couldn't be taken for granted.

At least not for him.

Though it was idiotic, he'd even walked into his house last night and imagined it being a real home. Imagined what it would be like to walk in the door with Judith by his side.

Or even better, he let himself daydream about walking into the house after a day out in the fields and seeing her pretty face . . . smiling, because she was waiting for him.

He'd be mortified if she'd ever guessed the things he was thinking. No doubt she'd be scared. Without a doubt, she'd take off running the next time she saw him walking her way.

Now, though, he could only look forward to seeing her for a few more days until Christmas. Then Mr. Graber was going to have more time to work, Judith's brother Joshua might finally be settled in his new home, the crowds would be gone, and they'd have no need for his help anymore.

Then, as soon as he got an offer on the house, he'd move on.

Looking at the clock above the kitchen sink, he frowned. Seven. He had hours before it was time to go to work. Since he was dressed and had eaten an hour earlier, he walked to his stack of library books and pulled out a new mystery.

Perhaps he could get halfway through it this morning. If he did, he'd have a reason to go back to the library after work.

Anything would be better than sitting here alone with only memories for company. Again.

* * *

He'd waited until a quarter after nine to walk to the store. Along the way he stopped and listened to a quartet of *Englischer* carolers singing about white Christmases, and even helped himself to a mug of hot cider and a slice of warm gingerbread, fresh out of the oven at the Sugarcreek Inn.

Then, promptly at five minutes to ten, he entered the front of the shop.

"Ben, you are right on time!" Mr. Graber said from his position behind the cash register. Still not looking up, he added, "We are glad to see you, too. Your hands are sorely needed. I don't know when we've ever been so busy."

"I thought merchants were happy about busy stores," Ben teased as he strode forward.

"Oh, for sure that is a fact. It's just that a man can only do so much with two hands, you know?"

"Yes, Mr. Graber. I know." After looking briefly at Judith, who was back behind the bakery case helping a pair of women pick out iced Christmas cutouts, Ben approached the counter. "Luckily, I have two hands to offer and I'm thankful for the work. What would you like me to do today?"

"There's much I'd like you to do, but I think all you're going to have time to do is wait on customers."

Ben was about to nod and venture closer to a group of *Englischers* looking at pine candles when Mr. Graber spoke again. "However, son, if you do have time, there's a slew of boxes in the back that need to be unpacked. Any chance you could do that after the customers leave?"

"Of course." Again, he stepped away, eager to be of use.

Mr. Graber spoke again. "If you *are* here late . . . there are lots of boxes that need to be broken down and carried to the Dumpsters. And shelves to be stocked. And deliveries to be made as well." Narrowing his eyes, he asked, "How late can you stay?"

With effort, Ben kept a straight face. Mr. Graber's crafty manner amused him. "As long as you need me."

"Truly?" His eyes lit up.

Ben nodded. After all, there was nothing else for him to do. Besides go to the library.

"Could you stay an hour or two after hours and help Judith restock?"

"Until eight o'clock or so?"

"*Jah.* I'd come back later and work but had promised Judith's *mamm* that I'd take her to the Wal-Mart tonight. We hired a driver so we could get a few things for Maggie and Toby."

"I don't mind staying, Mr. Graber. I'll stay here with Judith and restock as much as I can." Then, remembering how fearful he'd been when he thought of her being alone on the dark, snowy streets of Sugarcreek, he added firmly, "And then I will take her home as well."

Satisfaction glowed in Mr. Graber's eyes as he continued to make plans. "Ben, if you do that, you might as well stay with us for dinner."

"**Danke.**"

"Our Maggie will be glad to see you. All she talked about while she ate her oatmeal this morning was her new friend Ben. You know, after supper, it is mighty late. Too late to be out and about." He snapped his fingers. "I know! Why don't you just plan on sleeping in Joshua's old room?"

He grinned, obviously pleased with his newest suggestion.

"I'm sorry, I couldn't do that."

"*Nee?* Where else would you like to sleep in our home?" He frowned. "I'm afraid we don't have the basement furnished at this time . . ."

"*Nee,* it's not that. I just couldn't impose on your hospitality like that."

"You wouldn't be imposing, son. It's just a matter of making things easier on all of us."

"I'm afraid I don't understand . . ."

"Ben, it's like this," Mr. Graber said almost too carefully, as if he were speaking to a child of limited mental capacity. "We are used to a busy house. Mrs. Graber and I like having all the bedrooms filled. Plus, I can tell you that it would make my *frau verra* pleased to fuss over you. To make sure you're warm and settled."

No. Ben knew he wasn't going to be needing those things . . .

In a rush, Mr. Graber continued. Just as if he was stating facts instead of his opinions. "And then, of course, we're going to be worried about you gettin' on home late at night."

"I'll be fine—"

"And, well, you know, since it is Christmas, we're going to have to do the whole thing again tomorrow." Deceptively innocent sounding, Mr. Graber sighed. "All things considered, it would simply be easiest on all of us if you just stayed the night. If you only dropped off our Judith, you'd cause us grief to no end."

Ben felt flummoxed. How did one respond to an offer like this? He had so few experiences of such generosity to fall back on. "I don't want to cause you any grief," he muttered.

"I know you don't." As Judith's voice carried over the store, the older man glanced toward her. Then, almost wistfully, he added, "We like ya, Ben. We like you *verra* much. You seem to fit in just fine with our family."

Well, what could he say to that? "If you would like me to stay late here, of course I will. I will also be grateful for the meal and the bed." As soon as the words were out of his mouth, Ben ached to take them back. How pitiful did he sound? Clearing his throat, he added a bit more forcefully, "I mean . . . I could make it work. If you don't think Judith would mind?"

"Judith won't mind at all."

"I won't mind what?" Judith asked from just a few mere feet away. A line formed between her brows as she looked from her father to Ben and then back to her *daed* again.

Ben almost groaned aloud. Of course she would come here right at this moment, hearing her father offer him a meal and a bed. Just as if he had nowhere better to be.

However, instead of appearing awkward, Mr. Graber looked pleased as punch. "Judith, dear. I was suggesting to Ben that maybe he could spend the night at our house when he drops you off."

"He doesn't need to drop me off."

"Sure he does. 'Cause he's going to be working late with you this evening."

A pinched look appeared in between her brows. "How late?"

"Just until eight or so."

Right there and then, pure fire entered Judith's eyes. If Ben hadn't been so transfixed, he would have been wary. She looked mad enough to spit nails.

"You didn't ask *me* about working late tonight, Daed."

"I'm telling you now, daughter. What more do you want?"

Mr. Graber looked so clueless, and Judith so hurt, Ben ached to say something, anything, to make things right. But what could he say? This wasn't his business, and this wasn't his family. Really he was only a paid employee, and a temporary one at that.

For a brief moment, Ben thought Judith was going to challenge her father. Her lips pursed and she drew a breath. Ben paused, half hoping she would protest, just so he could see what she was like when she was angry. But then, looking around at the many customers milling around, she slumped. "Where will Ben sleep?" she asked softly.

Which, of course, hurt him more than any harsh words of condemnation. She looked resigned to her fate. No matter what.

So though he'd been determined not to get involved, he did. "You know, I surely don't have to do anything but drop off Judith—"

"You don't have to—"

"We want you to be with us," Mr. Graber

said firmly. Interrupting Judith's protest. Turning to his daughter, his voice had a new edge to it, one that surely brooked no argument. "Ben will be sleeping tonight in Joshua's old room. Daughter, you surely don't have a problem with this, do you? Surely you haven't forgotten how to be hospitable?"

Twin flags of red colored her cheeks. "Of course not."

And Ben noticed that she wasn't looking at him. He'd never felt like anyone's burden. But at the moment he definitely did.

But more than that, he refused to be the source of discomfort or pain for the woman he so admired. "You know what? It might be better if I just went home to my own place—"

"Nonsense. Right, Judith?"

"Right. We'd be happy to have you stay."

Did it matter if her words sounded wooden and forced?

"Well, now. I'm *verra* grateful that is all settled." Mr. Graber clapped his hands together. "All right, then. Now that our plans are made, I'm going to leave things in your four capable hands while I go back to the office and try to dig myself out from under a mountain of paperwork. After that, I'm going to the farm. Let me know if you need anything."

He turned before either of them could say a word.

Though the store was filled with customers in sweaters and coats, all chattering with each other, the space between him and Judith felt as if it was their own world. He wasn't aware of anyone else but her.

This could have been the setting for things that dreams are made of, but unfortunately all he felt was her extreme disapproval. Felt it all the way to his toes. He couldn't say he blamed her, either.

"Well, that was awkward," he said. "I'm sorry about all of this. I promise, I didn't invite myself to your home."

"Oh, Ben, I know you didn't."

Though he should have been assured, he wasn't. There was a note of sadness in her voice that he couldn't ignore. "Judith, what would you like me to do to get out of it? Say I can't work late?"

"You'd do that?"

"Of course I would. I'll do whatever you need me to do. The last thing I want is to force my company on you."

"It's not that I don't want to be with you, or to have you at our house, it's that my father never thinks to ask *me*. Sometimes I just get so sick and tired of always doing what's expected of me."

"I understand."

"Do you?" Those blue eyes of hers turned translucent, and he wasn't sure whether they were that way from her emotion or because tears were threatening to fall.

Just as he was about to admit that he'd had lots of experience of living without choices . . . that he'd acted up when he was young because he'd felt like he had no other outlet . . . they were interrupted by a customer.

"Excuse me?" a man in a bright blue parka called out. "Excuse me, I need some help over here. Hello?"

"We'd best get to work," Judith muttered.

"Indeed. But maybe we can talk more another time?"

"*Jah.* Sure . . ."

Taking advantage of the momentary burst of silence, a heavyset woman in a red sweatshirt from the other side of the store stepped up importantly. "I need help getting a trunk down," she said. "Can you help me?"

"Of course. I'll be glad to," Ben replied. He was sad to leave the discussion but thankful to have something else to do besides wish things were different between Judith and himself.

Or, if he was honest, wish that he was different. He did wish he hadn't lived the last ten years of his life pushing everything and everyone away. And wished Judith didn't look at him and remember his temper. Or the way he'd always gotten into trouble.

He shook his head as if to clear it. Those longings caught him off guard. He'd been sure he'd given up all desire for the things he couldn't have years ago.

Chapter Ten

Six Days Until Christmas

"I was so happy to see you this morning, Caleb," Mrs. Miller said as she bustled around the kitchen and sliced him a large square of warm applesauce cake. "Seeing you sitting here in my kitchen always brightens my day."

Eating Mrs. Miller's baked goods always brightened his day, Caleb reflected. A longtime innkeeper, she was truly one of the best bakers in Sugarcreek.

As she brought him the warm treat, now liberally topped with a dollop of fresh whipped cream, he looked up at her fondly. "You didn't know I was comin'? You just happened to be baking my favorite cake this morning?"

She squeezed his shoulder with a laugh. "Caleb Graber, don't you think I know you well by now? You've never had a favorite treat! You love them all."

Sure enough, as he took the first bite, Caleb knew she spoke the truth. He dearly loved everything that came from Mrs. Miller's kitchen. Into everything she incorporated a liberal dose of love and care. If he was honest, he'd say he liked being in the kitchen, too. She collected snowmen—figurines and images—and in December, it seemed everything in the room was or displayed a smiling white snowman. "This is wonderful, Mrs. Miller."

"You are a dear to say such sweet things. I'll send some home with you for your parents."

"*Danke,* but I'm afraid I can't take any today."

"Ah, yes. You're meeting Rebecca here, aren't you?"

"*Jah.*" He took another bite quickly so he wouldn't be tempted to ask more about

Rebecca. It wouldn't be right to ask for private information about the girl he liked so much. He didn't know much about relationships, but even he knew it was only right to wait for her to tell him her secrets.

After crossing the room, Mrs. Miller pulled out one of the sturdy black Windsor chairs next to him. Holding a piping hot mug of coffee in between her wide palms, she spoke. "Knowing Rebecca has been a joy for me. Not only is she a tremendous help with this old place, but she's a wonderful-*gut* girl, Caleb. You are lucky to have her."

Her frank words caused him to flinch. "I don't 'have' her. I just like her." *A lot,* he added silently. Caleb eyed the remaining portion of his cake. Only two, maybe three bites remained. With care, he speared a bite, hoping to make it last longer. After taking another sip of her coffee, Mrs. Miller got to her feet again. With a smile, she picked up his plate and carried it back to the counter. There, she cut off another sizable portion of cake, then brought it back to him, this time the bowl of cold whipped cream in her other hand. "Here you go,

Caleb. I wasn't sure how much whipped cream to put on your piece this time."

"Any amount would do."

"Yes, but you might as well have what you want, don't you agree? It's important for a man to know what he wants."

He stilled, his finger tightening on the spoon in the whipped cream. "What I want isn't the only thing that matters," he said slowly, realizing they were now talking about so much more than just his appetite for desserts. "Sometimes it's necessary to know what is right."

"I'm glad to hear you say that." She sat back down. "You see, when Rebecca started working here, not only was it a real blessing to me—the job was a blessing for her as well."

For her? There was obviously a story there. Caleb ached to ask what it was but yet again fought off the urge to pry. Rebecca would tell him more when the time was right.

He had to believe that.

Luckily the back door opened and in came Rebecca, immediately brightening his world. Today she wore a teal dress and thick-soled black boots. The dress's fabric brightened her skin and made her eyes seem even bluer than usual.

Without thinking, he got to his feet and walked to her. "*Gut matin,* Becca."

As he'd hoped, her eyes glowed when they lit on him. "Hi, Caleb." After smiling at him again, she turned to Mrs. Miller. "*Gut matin,* Mrs. Miller."

Caleb noticed the woman didn't get to her feet. Instead, she simply smiled fondly at Rebecca.

"Help yourself to some cake, dear. And I put out some orange slices for you, too."

Rebecca approached the refrigerator as if the lady had hidden a secret treasure there. "Oh, look at those oranges. They look beautiful."

"Eat them all, Rebecca. And Caleb will serve you cake." She looked at Caleb meaningfully. "Right?"

"Sure. I'll be happy to." Now he was the one bustling around the kitchen, waiting on his girl. Rebecca sat down and ate one succulent slice of orange after the other, just like she'd never tasted anything so good.

Moments later, she took a bite of the

cake, but it was obvious to even him that gingerbread cake wasn't nearly as delicious to her as the succulent fruit.

When they were almost done, Mrs. Miller left the room, then returned with a large box filled with stacks of neatly wrapped braided bread. "Here you two go. I hope all your recipients will enjoy the bread."

Rebecca got to her feet and carefully picked up one of the packages. "These look mighty fine. I'm sure they will be much appreciated."

"As long as they are enjoyed, I will feel blessed. Truly, that is all that matters to me."

"Where should we go next, Rebecca?" Caleb asked.

"To your house, I suppose. Anson is going to be accompanying us. Or have you forgotten?"

"I told him not to." At her look of confusion, he added, "There's no need for him to come. I promise you that."

"I don't mind if he joins us, Caleb," she said softly.

"I do."

"And why is that?"

"No particular reason," he hedged.

"Hmm." Her eyes twinkled. Making it so obvious that she was biting her tongue in order not to tease him anymore.

Caleb kept his mouth shut, too. He didn't want to shock her with what was really on his mind. Because what he wanted to say was that he didn't want to share her. When he was around Rebecca, he didn't want there to be another person within a hundred feet of them.

He wanted to be the only person to hold her hand or to steady her elbow when they walked down stairs. He wanted to be the only person to wrap an arm around her shoulders.

Selfishly, he wanted all her words and smiles to be only for him. For the blush on her cheeks to be because of something he said.

But of course, none of that could be admitted. They were young. And he still got the sense that she was hiding something from him.

Therefore, he kept his answer easy. "Whatever you want, I will do," he said.

And for that, he got his reward.

Rebecca smiled at him like he'd just

raised the sun from the horizon and brightened her day.

By 5:30 that evening, Judith knew she was having a terribly hard time keeping her feelings in line. Never before had she been so aware of another person as she was with Ben Knox. No matter what he did or where he was, she sensed his presense. With Ben, it was as if she had some sixth sense where he was concerned.

Knowing that he looked just as aware of her should have given her some comfort. It didn't. All it did was make her remember their differences. He had skipped school when she'd tried her best. Rumor had it that he'd done all kinds of sinful things during his *rumspringa,* whereas she'd told her parents she didn't need any time to decide her future.

Now, though, when he looked at her through hooded eyes, she wished she'd had more experiences with boys and dating. Then she would be able to understand more of what his looks and words meant.

Lowering her eyelids, she snuck a peek at him through the corner of one eye.

When he noticed her gaze, he stilled. "Everything all right?"

As a matter of fact, it was not. Her stomach was in knots and it felt like monster butterflies had joined the knots, too. "Everything's fine. Do you, ah, need some help?"

"Do I need help sweeping? I don't think so."

She wasn't sure if he was teasing her or not. "I didn't mean just sweeping. Do you need anything . . . ?"

"I don't need a thing, Judith." Looking at the floor, he began to sweep again.

Judith doubted he'd ever felt weak or unsure in his life.

As a thick lock of dark hair brushed his brow, she watched it sway against his skin—and was looking at him in a way that she hadn't been able to stop doing for hours. It seemed no matter how busy she was, or how many customers she was serving, her attention always returned to him.

What was she going to do when he left after Christmas?

Well, at least she could ask him about that. "Ben?"

"Hmm?"

"Ben, after Christmas, what are you going to do?"

"Leave Sugarcreek. Well, I will as soon as someone buys the house."

She closed her eyes, remembering the sign she'd seen in front of his home. "Then what will you do? Where will you go?"

"I'm not sure yet."

Honestly, could he ever just give her information without her begging and prodding for it? "Will you visit family?"

A muscle in his jaw jumped. "No."

"Then what—"

The door chime rang as a crowd of tourists burst inside. "Miss? Miss, can you help us?" one lady in a sweatshirt decorated with a large Santa Claus called out.

"Yes, of course," Judith replied. "What can I help you with?"

"We need some baked goods. And Trail bologna." One lady held out a list. "We need a lot of things. I'm giving an open house tomorrow and I'm hopelessly behind. I know you're going to close soon, but if you could stay open just a little longer, you'll save my life."

"I'll help you get everything."

"And I'll help, too," Ben said as he walked to her side.

One of the younger women gazed at Ben like she'd caught the grand prize at a county fair. "If you could help me, I would be most grateful."

"Lead the way," he said with a smile.

Judith felt jealousy rise inside her. Embarrassed, she tamped it down. But still couldn't help but keep an eye on him.

Probably because most of her brain seemed to be taking a vacation!

Over and again, she would hear his voice through the perimeter of her thoughts. Then, just like a wisp of smoke from a fire, little by little his words would drift toward her. Muddling and mingling with her thoughts. Those words would get in the way of the conversations she had with customers and with the train of her thoughts. As she'd hear his voice or his laugh, she'd still. And only think of him.

It was fairly disturbing.

What was she going to do when Ben was at her house, sleeping down the hall? Surely, she'd go crazy!

Since that wasn't acceptable, she vowed

to work extra hard to keep her feelings to herself. If her family ever caught sight of her gazing at him like she was doing at the store, they would never let her hear the end of it. And it would be no less than she deserved.

She'd been too reserved all her life.

To her shame, she'd even looked down upon others who wore their emotions for anyone to see.

She'd been disdainful of the way Caleb wore every emotion on his sleeve. Of Anson's penchant for focusing on his wishes instead of his chores. To her shame, she'd even lost patience with Joshua a time or two. She'd thought his struggle over his future had been a bit silly, especially when it had been painfully obvious that Josh and Gretta were perfect for each other.

By 6:30, after Ben finally shooed the last of their customers out, her nerves felt like they'd been stretched so thin they were about to break and snap. Now she was going to have to suffer through two hours of being alone with him in the store? After, she was going to have to sit by his side in an enclosed buggy. There, in the closed confines, their cold breath would mingle and their bodies would brush against each other. Attempting to stay calm, cool, and collected seemed an insurmountable task.

As the ridiculous bird clock chirped above them, Judith felt her stomach knot.

And then Ben chuckled.

"What?"

"Sorry, did I startle you? Were you gathering wool?"

Well, she'd been gathering all her thoughts about *him*. Not that that was anything new . . .

Ben continued. "I was laughing at the man who just left. Can you believe that guy bought ten pounds of pecans and five baskets?"

Trying to recall what the man had looked like, though of course she couldn't, Judith nodded weakly.

He grinned. "I never imagined nuts would make a *gut* gift, but he seemed right proud of himself. When he started talking about his favorite ways to eat them, I had to bite the inside of my mouth to keep from smiling."

"I've given up trying to second-guess what people are interested in," she agreed. "One thing is for sure, though, they're likin' everything we've got. I don't remember a better December for sales." Yes, this was the way to do it! She simply needed to keep the conversation only about business.

"What would you like me to do for you?"

He was standing so close she felt her breath catch. Forced herself to remember that Ben was talking about work. Not anything else.

"Maybe you could go around the aisles and pick up a bit. Also, please look and see if you notice anything that we've just about run out of. Later we can restock."

"I can do that."

Judith busied herself with counting money and receipts, trying not to be too hard on herself when she continued to count the same stack of dollar bills over and over again.

When Ben came back toward her, he carried a list in his right hand.

Unable to stop herself, she watched him approach. His shoulders were broad and, as usual, there wasn't a bit of hesitancy in the way he moved.

Once again, she recalled gaping at him during their last year in school together.

And remembered the way he'd raised a brow when he'd caught her doing so.

In a flash, the memories rushed back, just as if it had been yesterday. They'd been on the playground, and for once she was sitting by herself. He'd been bouncing a basketball on the blacktop . . . and she hadn't been able to stop staring at him.

"Did no one ever teach you manners, Judith Graber?" he'd asked. She'd hated that she'd been so rude, and had hated even more that he'd noticed. "The last thing I need is a lesson in manners from you."

"Doubt that."

Her head had popped up. "Why?"

"Because every single time I turn around, I see you staring at me like I am stained," he replied, his voice turning husky.

She'd felt her cheeks heating. "I don't. I mean, I don't think you're stained."

"I think you do."

"Nee—"

Four steps brought him close. So close, he stopped a mere foot away from her. "I know what I see. I know what you

see when you look at me. You know I'm not good enough."

Her mouth had gone dry as she'd attempted to say the right words back. To tell him that though she was a little afraid of him, she'd thought that maybe, just maybe, he wasn't as bad as they'd all thought.

Though the school yard was almost empty, she'd felt on display. And, like the silly girl she was, she'd started worrying more about what their teacher would think instead of focusing on Ben.

Who had been staring at her with his beautiful hazel eyes that were framed too well with dark eyelashes.

Who always smelled clean and masculine and wonderful.

Just as she continued to stand there, painfully awkward, he leaned close. So close, if she'd lifted her chin and swayed forward, their lips would meet. "Do ya want to know a secret, Judith?"

She hadn't been able to help herself. She nodded.

Looking satisfied, he lowered his head slightly, so his lips brushed her

ear. "I don't mind. Feel free to stare at me all you want."

She'd been so shocked, so embarrassed, her hands had curved into fists.

Then she'd turned and ran home. His deep laughter floating behind her.

Even when she remembered the scene now, Judith felt herself cringe. She'd been hopelessly naïve, and he'd used that innocence to his advantage. During their last months of school together, she'd avoided him as much as she could.

And when other boys had given her attention, she'd gone walking with them when they'd asked.

It was only late at night, when she couldn't sleep, that she remembered just how much she'd once fancied Ben Knox. Before he'd embarrassed her.

And before she'd known better than to risk her heart on someone so outrageous. Someone so unsuitable for a goody-two-shoes like Judith Graber.

Chapter Eleven

Six Days Until Christmas

"We haven't gone out to dinner in ages," Lilly told Robert as she drove him down Main Street toward the Sugarcreek Inn. "I'm so excited."

With what could only be described as exaggerated patience, her husband sighed. "Lilly, if you want to go out to eat more, you only have to ask."

"I don't want to."

"Perhaps you do . . . sometimes?"

Well, she did, every now and then. Sometimes her feet and back hurt after waitressing for hours. On those days it was hard to find the energy to come home and spend more time in the kitchen.

Especially since no matter how hard she tried, the food she made wasn't all that good. Correction. It wasn't good at all. But none of those reasons were enough to stop trying. "I wouldn't do that to you. I know you like to have supper waiting for you when you get home from the factory."

"I like having you home," he corrected gently. "That is what is important to me. *You're* who I look forward to seeing. Not a roast chicken."

"I know that. I mean, so far I've managed to ruin every chicken dinner I attempted."

"The last one wasn't so bad."

"It was far from good." When she stopped at the stoplight, she glanced his way. Robert was obviously trying hard not to smile.

Which made her finally relax. When she thought of all the meals she'd made for him that had been barely edible, she began to giggle. "I'm afraid to bake fish again."

"Perhaps that's for the best . . ."

"But I do think my lasagna has improved. Slightly."

"It has gotten much better, that is true. Still, we can go out to eat a little more often. Perhaps once a week?"

She would love that. But still . . . "I just don't want you to change your life for me. Even though, you know, you already have."

"You wouldn't be doing anything to me. You'd be happy. And I like making you happy." Gently, he looked her way and smiled. Looking down the street, his expression turned tense. "Of course, you didn't have to choose this restaurant. We could have gone to Dutch Valley. Or maybe even Mexican food."

"I wanted to come here."

"Even though you work here?"

"Even though."

Her heart skittered a bit as she felt the full force of his attention. Recently, he'd shaved his beard. Now he was as clean-shaven as any *Englischer*. The new look made him look younger.

And, perhaps, more a match to her?

Like a reoccurring dream, the old nerves and self-doubts grabbed ahold of her again. "Do you miss your beard?"

"Not at all. I like my cheeks smooth." His

hand went right to his chin. "What made you ask that?"

"I don't know. I just thought that maybe you wanted to grow it again."

"I don't." He smiled slightly. Then, right when she was at a traffic light, he leaned close and kissed her cheek. "I could have sworn my wife liked my smooth cheeks."

She couldn't believe it, and blushed. Robert was filled with surprises for her. Always. In so many ways, the perceptions she'd had about the way an Amish man behaved, or the way he might treat her, constantly went on its ear.

Robert was as affectionate and sweet as any newlywed she'd ever seen. He was eager to hold her in his arms at night; and when they were alone, he touched her often.

He continually put her needs first.

After brushing his lips against her jawline, he sat back in his seat. "Lilly? Aren't you going to tell me what you think of my smooth cheeks?"

"You know I love your smooth cheeks," she admitted with a shy smile.

"Then stop worrying, wife." Stretching out his legs, now encased in jeans instead of homemade wool pants, he slapped a hand on his thigh. "Though this adjustment hasn't been easy, there are some things I'm enjoying. One of them is my smooth cheeks. Another is my new clothes. These jeans are mighty comfortable."

Secretly, she'd been missing her jeans, though she had to admit she was getting more used to the conservative dresses she was wearing now. She'd also been missing mascara and wearing her hair down.

When she turned into the inn's parking lot, she was happy to see how full it was. "They've got a good crowd here tonight. I bet Mrs. Kent will be happy about that."

"You sound almost wistful. Do you wish you worked more often?"

"Not at all. I'm happy with my three days a week."

"Are you sure?" There was enough of an edge in Robert's voice to make Lilly realize she wasn't the only one who needed reassurance.

Reaching out, she squeezed his hand. "I'm happy with you, Robert. I'm happier with you than I could dream possible. And that's enough for me."

Looking at her more closely, he finally nodded. "You mean that, don't you?"

"I do." She parked the car, climbed out, and waited for him to come around.

Then they went in together, side by side. Just like every other married couple. "What are you going to get to eat?"

"I'm not sure."

Almost immediately, Miriam came rushing forward. "Lilly! Look at you! What are you doing here?"

Glancing shyly Robert's way, Lilly shrugged. "Eating supper out."

More than one tableful of customers turned her way and smiled at the commotion. A few of the regulars raised their hands. "Lilly! Good to see you."

She couldn't help beaming. "Thank you! It's good to be here." As she gazed around the restaurant, she couldn't help but grin at the line of Christmas cards hanging from ribbons over the windows and the small artificial tree the girls had set up near the back.

Though she still worked during the day, the restaurant felt different at night. Quiet instrumental music played in the background, red-and-green checkered tablecloths decorated each table, and strands of Christmas lights lined the ceiling.

"We miss seeing your smiles," an elderly lady said. "When are you on the schedule again?"

"Monday."

"If you want extra hours, let me know," Miriam said. "Things around here have been crazy."

After darting a look in Robert's direction, she shrugged. "I don't know. I'm a pretty busy wife now you know."

"We know," Mrs. Kent said as she walked over to greet them as well. "I saw Irene Graber and your mother in here the other day. They take great pride in letting me know what a dutiful wife you've become."

Squeezing her shoulder, Robert chuckled. "Lilly is a *gut* wife. She makes me happy."

Miriam held two menus to her chest. "Are you ready to be seated?"

"Definitely," Lilly said.

"Your usual table, Robert?" Miriam asked with a sly smile.

"What table is that?"

"The one by the window, of course. You always came in and sat there when you were trying to get up the nerve to court our Lilly."

Right before her eyes, Robert blushed.

"We'll take a seat over in the back by the Christmas tree. Thanks, Miriam," Lilly said.

Robert waited until she took a seat, then sat across from her. "Is this why you wanted to come here?" he asked. His voice was gentle but his gaze was suspicious. "Because you want to work more and you think I needed encouragement?"

"No." Though hearing she was missed did feel good, working was the furthest thing from her mind at the moment.

"Are you sure? Because it kind of seems that way."

Lilly heard the challenge in his voice. And a thread of disappointment—because he feared she was lying. "I promise you, Robert. I didn't not want to come here in order to work more hours. I'm simply comfortable here, that's all."

He waited a moment, then nodded. "All right."

After asking Miriam for two glasses of iced tea, they sat in an uncomfortable silence while they waited for her to return. The air between them felt awkward.

After another moment's pause, Robert looked down at the menu and studied it intently. Lilly did the same, just as if she'd never worked here and didn't have feelings about what she liked and didn't like.

"I think I'll get smothered chicken," she finally said.

"I'll get the same thing," he replied.

Miriam came and took their orders. With a curious look, she took Lilly's menu. Lilly averted her eyes, not wanting to see Miriam's confusion because she knew it echoed her own feelings.

Because as each minute passed, Robert was drifting away from her. In truth, his behavior was like night and day from the man kissing her cheek at the stoplight.

And just when she thought things couldn't get any worse, the front door opened and in walked Abe, Abe's wife, Mary, and his father.

They saw her and Robert. Glared. And then, after a moment's hesitation, the trio approached. Across from her, she sensed Robert's discomfort. Though his relatives' appearance wasn't her fault, she still felt responsible for their dinner out getting worse. Why in the world had she ever imagined that this would be a good idea?

"Robert? Evening," his father said as they approached. "How goes it?"

"We are fine. *Danke*."

Lilly raised her head. Waited for the newcomers to acknowledge her. But just like when she'd first met them at the flea market, none of the three even looked her way.

It was almost like she didn't exist.

Which completely broke her heart. Not for herself; she was used to straddling two worlds. But Robert surely wasn't.

After it became obvious that his family wasn't going to say a word to her, Robert stood abruptly, his chair scraping the floor as he did so.

"Perhaps we could speak outside for a moment," he said. Then he walked to the door, not even bothering to put on his coat.

Not even bothering to offer a word of explanation to her.

Mr. Miller looked at her. "Lilly," he said, with a nod. Then turned and followed his son. After another few seconds, Abe followed the other two men.

Mary went and sat down.

"What is going on?" Miriam asked when she approached with a pitcher to refill Lilly's glass of water. "Is everything all right?"

She didn't have the heart to pretend it was. "No."

Miriam sat in Robert's empty seat. "What can I do to help?"

"Nothing. There's nothing to do," she murmured, watching Robert and Abe exchange heated words right in front of the picture windows. To her dismay, she wasn't the only one watching the conversation with interest. No, the Miller family seemed to capture the interest of just about everyone in the restaurant. Two ladies were eating their rolls while unabashedly attempting to read the men's lips.

Lilly grimaced. She ached to fix everything between Robert and his family, but she had no idea how to do it.

Miriam got to her feet and squeezed Lilly's shoulder. "I know things seem bad, but they'll get better."

"I don't see how."

"Anyone with eyes can see that you and Robert were meant to be together. Our Lord wouldn't have put you in each other's path if He hadn't intended for you to be together."

"You really believe that, don't you?"

Miriam nodded. "And I'm not the only one, Lilly. There are a lot of us Amish who have no desire to shun Robert."

"No offense, but I wish Robert's cousin was one of them."

Miriam's eyes twinkled. "Let me tell ya a secret. Abe Miller didn't just start being narrow-minded and full of spite. I do believe he's had a lot of practice over the years. Now, I'll go get your food."

Lilly almost asked her to wait, but as a waitress there, she knew that wouldn't be fair to either Miriam or the cooks. They had a lot of food to make and serve and couldn't be dependent on the soap opera that her marriage was turning out to be.

"I'm sorry about that," Robert said when he returned to his seat. "I simply couldn't hold my tongue any longer."

Lilly could practically feel dark emotions emanate from him. "What did you say?"

"I'll tell you later," he said as Miriam approached with two heaping plates of pan-roasted chicken, mashed potatoes, green beans, and tomato gravy. "Ah. This looks mighty good, Miriam."

"I'll let the girls in the back know," she replied with a smile before turning away.

After two forkfuls, Robert looked at Lilly. "Now, wasn't there something you'd wanted to talk to me about?"

"Nothing of importance," she whispered. Suddenly, she didn't trust her voice, his ears, or their audience. The last thing he needed was for her to once again share her worries about not being good enough.

He might already think that.

Chapter Twelve

Six Days Until Christmas

"Sorry," Ben muttered under his breath as the buggy lurched forward after sliding a bit on a small patch of snow.

Though the main roads had been fairly clear, their driveway was another story. The packed snow was easy for the horse to cover but not nearly as easy for the buggy.

The horse's hooves crunched along and the buggy rocked a bit as Ben attempted to stay in the wheel ruts that had since formed on the long driveway to the house.

"S'okay, *Gual,*" he murmured. "S'okay."

As if Beauty understood, her gait smoothed out and they were on their way again.

Beside him, Judith was tempted to grasp Ben's arm. Not to steady herself but to reassure him. This was the first time she could ever remember him not doing anything with his trademark confidence. This new vulnerability he was exhibiting both caught her off guard and drew her closer to him. Just as it was becoming terribly obvious that he was worried about being at their home.

The whole way home she'd wanted to say something to him about it, but in the end kept her peace. Time and again, Caleb and Joshua had criticized her for coming off as a bit of a know-it-all, and that was the last way she wanted Ben to think of her.

But when he finally reined in Beauty and they stopped at the barn's entrance, Judith knew she had to say something. It was only right.

"Do you wish you would have said no?" she asked quietly. "Do you wish you would have refused my father's offer?"

For a moment, it looked as if he was fighting an internal battle. Then he looked at her. *"Nee,"* he finally said, his lips pursed.

The full moon's glow on the snow on the ground created an otherworldly quality, and the faint lights shining through the windows of her home cast an illuminating sheen over both of them. Bathing them with soft light.

She'd never been so glad of the moon before. If not for that, she didn't think she would have been able to spy the skepticism that flashed in his eyes.

"For what it's worth, I'm glad you're staying."

"For what it's worth, huh?" A secret flared in his expression. One that she would have paid money in order to understand. "Judith Graber, I don't know how to tell you this, but I guess I'll do my best. When you speak, I listen. Your opinion means a lot to me."

He turned away then, opened his door, and hopped out. After she did the same, he guided Beauty into the barn and proceeded to unharness her.

Judith walked to his side and took the mare's bridle. When she tried to do more, he stopped her with a hand. "*Nee,* Judith. I'll do this. Go inside where it's warm."

"But I can't let you care for Beauty by yourself."

"It's no trouble."

"But—"

He faced her. "Judith, if you are concerned, ask Anson or Caleb to come out and help. But I'm not going to let you stand in this cold barn a moment longer."

"I'm fine—"

"Go inside and get warm. Please."

She turned away and followed his directions, hearing his words float in her head, bringing with them tender feelings that felt almost unfamiliar.

Well, outside of her dreams.

The moment she stepped into the house, she walked into the kitchen.

Her mother, sitting at the table and working on a puzzle, looked up at her with a smile. "You're home. *Gut*. And where is Ben?"

"He's taking care of Beauty. But he needs help."

"Couldn't you help him?"

"He asked for Caleb or Anson."

"Or Anson?" A line formed between her mother's brows. "He's too young for that, don't you think? He's only . . ."

"Nine."

She blinked. "Ah, yes. I suppose Joshua was doing chores like that at nine, hmm?" Getting to her feet, she walked to the living room and told Anson to go help Ben.

Judith stood quietly as she heard Anson complain a bit, then ultimately, he dashed beside her, threw on boots and a coat, and scampered out to the barn.

Her mother came back in, a satisfied expression on her face. "I'm right pleased with that Ben. It was good of him to ask for Anson. We all forget that boy needs more responsibilities." She paused then, no doubt noticing Judith's pink cheeks. "Perhaps you'd care to take off your cloak now, daughter? I've kept two dinners waiting on you."

"Yes, Mamm." Judith turned away before her mother could think to ask about her pink cheeks. Or anything else.

"Ben, how come you asked for me?" Anson asked as he stood by him and carefully brushed Beauty.

Looking down at the wiry boy at his side, Ben fought a smile. "Why wouldn't I?"

"You don't think I'm too small?"

"To help with a *gual*? Of course not."

"How come you didn't want Judith to help you?"

"Because she's been working all day."

"But so have you."

"Judith is a woman." There. Surely that was answer enough? Honestly, Ben was starting to think that maybe people didn't ask Anson to do things not because they didn't think he could do that work . . . but rather because they didn't want to hear the thousand questions that never seemed to stop erupting from the child.

"Everyone else asks Judith to do stuff."

"Well, I am not everyone." Furthermore, if he'd had his way, Judith would be doing a whole lot less.

But of course her schedule wasn't his business.

After rubbing Beauty's neck and then giving her a few scratches between her ears, Ben led the horse to her stall. "Do you have her feed ready?"

"Yep." In short order, Anson put a good

armful of hay in Beauty's feed trough, followed by a cup of oats.

Beauty dug in with relish. Ben chuckled with Anson as they watched the horse enjoy her dinner.

With the horse now taken care of, Ben pushed himself away from the wooden stall. "I guess it's my turn to eat now, huh?"

"*Jah.* My *mamm*'s got a plate ready for you."

The consideration humbled him. Though it wasn't any of his business, he still went ahead and spoke. "And Judith? Did your *mamm* fix a plate for her, too?"

Anson tilted his head at him. "Well, yes. To be sure. Why wouldn't she?"

Ben knew why he'd asked it—because his parents had been masters at putting company's needs first and his last. But he wasn't about to utter that. "No reason," he said as they walked out of the barn, stopping to fasten the latch behind them. "I tell you what, Anson. I think I'm going to sleep real good tonight."

"Me, too." Almost circumspectly, Anson watched Ben stretch his arms, and then did the same exact motion.

Ben hid a smile as they continued walking on the snow. The boy's hero worship amused him—and gave him pause, too. To his recollection, no one had ever thought he was good enough to imitate.

The fact that Anson was doing so made him mildly uncomfortable; and though it was probably not good, it fueled his pride, too.

When they were almost to the house, Anson glanced his way. "My *daed* said you're going to be sleeping at our house a lot now."

"He said that?"

"Uh-huh. You'll be in Joshua's old room."

"Is that near yours?"

"Nope. I'm with Caleb." Anson stopped and pointed to a few darkened windows on the second story. "You're right next to Judith."

"Right next to her, huh?"

"Yep." Anson looked at him strangely. "Is there something wrong with that?"

"Not at all." Other than, well, he knew he was going to act like a fool and think about Judith sleeping in her bed with just a thin wall in between them.

Of course, every one of those thoughts was wrong. Seeking to lighten things up, he said, "Nothing's wrong. Unless Judith snores. Does she?"

"I don't think so," Anson said as they walked onto the front porch, then opened the front door. "But I can ask her for ya."

Hastily, Ben grabbed the door and pulled off his snowy boots in the front entryway. When Anson didn't seem in the mood to do the same, Ben quickly said, "Anson, there's no need to ask—"

"Judith! Hey, Judith," Anson called out. "Ben wants to know if you snore. Do you?"

"I do not," she called out from the kitchen.

Judith sounded horrified. If Ben could have turned right back around, he would have.

But because he had no choice, he stepped forward, following Anson's path into the kitchen. Now he felt even more of an interloper. An outsider.

When he entered the sunny kitchen, he swallowed hard as not only Judith stared at him, but Anson and their mother, too. "I was just teasin', Anson," he said weakly.

Anson screwed up his forehead. "I don't think so. We were talking about where he would sleep and he asked. Right, Ben?"

Ben didn't know what to say now. Judith

must have not either, because she seemed to only have eyes for the food on her plate.

But luckily Mrs. Graber was an expert at dealing with Anson. "Don't pay him no mind, Ben. Our Anson always says what's in his brain, for better or worse. Take your plate and go sit down, now."

After washing up, Ben took a seat next to Judith. After quietly giving thanks, not only for the food and Mrs. Graber's loving hands, but also their hospitality, he dug in.

As he'd expected, the chicken dinner was hot and filling and filled with comfort foods that he'd rarely had the occasion to enjoy. "This is mighty *gut,* Mrs. Graber."

"I'm glad you like it."

Carefully, he cut into another portion with his knife and fork. Determined to eat and then get on to bed.

Mr. Graber entered the room and sat down on Ben's other side. "Don't be eating in such a hurry now, son. You've got cake to eat, too."

"Cake?"

"Applesauce cake. Judith made it," he said with a fond look at Judith.

Ben stared at her in surprise. "When did you have time to bake a cake?"

"Before I went to work a few days ago," she said, her lips twitching. "Don't look so surprised. It wasn't hard to do."

"Our Judith is wonderful in the kitchen," her mother said. "She's been helping me for years."

There really was only one thing to say. "I'll be eager to taste your cake, Judith."

Her head whipped toward him. A heat shone in her eyes before she hid it. "I hope you will enjoy the treat," she said stiffly. Then before he could attempt to say another word to her, she got up and rinsed off her plate.

Ben couldn't help but watch her. Amazed yet again at all her talents. Here, she'd worked as hard as he had today, even staying late in order to restock.

Now, snug in her home, she was helping her mother without complaint, washing dishes and slicing cake. Then, to his amazement, she brought out a container of Cool Whip and placed a generous helping of whipped cream on top of each piece.

He stuffed a forkful of beans in his mouth so he wouldn't do something dumb and compliment her. But though his mouth was full, it certainly didn't stop his eyes from watching her every move. Thinking how graceful and feminine she was.

Thinking how pretty she was, even after a long day's work . . .

"So what do you think, Ben? Should we go ahead and plan on that?" Mr. Graber asked.

Ben blinked. He'd been so caught up in watching Judith he'd been completely ignoring his host. "I'm sorry. I think my mind drifted . . ."

But instead of berating him as his own father would have done, Mr. Graber just looked at him kindly. "I bet you are tired. No matter. All I was talking about was whether you thought we should put some more of the baskets on sale? We might lose a bit of the profits, but I think the increase in sales would only help the Care and Share project."

Care and Share was an organization to help Amish born with mental handicaps. "I think you are right." Then, worried he was overstepping his bounds, he looked at Judith, who had just approached them with two plates of cake, one for her father, one for him. "What do you think, Judith?"

She stilled. "I agree as well," she said

softly as she first handed her father a slice of cake, then walked to Ben's side.

"Judith, will you have some cake as well?"

"Not tonight. I'm afraid I'm too tired to eat much more."

If they'd had a different relationship, he would have circled his fingers around her wrist and pulled her closer. Maybe even pulled her onto his lap, where he could give her a hug and encourage her to rest against him.

Then, when she'd finally settled, he would have rubbed her back and told her how wonderful she was . . .

"Are you going to eat, Ben?"

Great. Once again, he'd been caught with his mind drifting, staring at Judith and thinking about things that were never going to be.

"I am," he said, picking up his fork and digging in. "This is *gut*."

"I'm glad you like it," Mr. Graber said expansively.

"*Gut naught*. I'm going to sleep," Judith said, leaving them quickly.

As her parents wished her pleasant dreams, Ben continued to eat. It was probably a very good idea to try to be a bit more distant. After all, Judith was a woman far better than he deserved.

All his life, everyone had told him so. And though he'd never been one to let others see his pain, the jibes had stuck with him. Even after all this time.

Chapter Thirteen

Five Days Until Christmas

Ben had quick reactions, and that was a fact. The moment Judith ran into him in the hall, he'd reached out and held her shoulders steady. "Easy, there."

She didn't need a mirror to know she was blushing. She could practically feel the blood rush to her cheeks as they stood too close together. "I'm sorry," she blurted.

Of course, she didn't move a step away, either. What was wrong with her?

His grip loosened, but he didn't drop his hands. Actually, he looked happy to stand there in the hall with her, exchanging greetings. "It's all right. I should have looked where I was going."

"It's my fault." She hadn't been thinking about much except for reaching her goal: the bathroom sink. She'd been eager to wash her face and brush her teeth before he saw her.

But now the worst had just happened. He was standing chest to chest with her. Looking at her way too closely.

Ach! With a bold step to her right, she pulled herself out of his grip and reached a hand out toward the door. "I'll see you downstairs. I just need to . . . um . . . get ready."

"I'll see you then." He winked at her. Winked!

Then turned and walked away. Whistling.

"Do you want the bathroom now? Or do you want to watch his backside for another few minutes?"

Judith turned on her heel and glared hard at her brother. "Caleb, hush!"

He crossed his arms over his chest. "Sorry. I'm just saying what I see . . . which is you staring at Ben Knox. Again."

"I wasn't staring. Much," she added when his raised his eyebrows.

"I didn't say nothing was wrong with it. Just teasing ya."

"I know." She glanced back down the hall. When she was satisfied that Ben was out of earshot, she looked at Caleb. "Do you think Ben and I would be a bad couple?"

"Are you courting?"

"*Nee.* But if we were . . ."

"I suppose he'd be a fine match for you. If any man wanted to put up with your bossy nature."

"You're not much help."

"Sorry. I've got my own relationships to think about."

"Is Rebecca giving you problems?"

"No. But I think she's hiding something from me."

"Like what?" Caleb's problems were far easier to concentrate on than hers.

"I don't have any idea. It's just a feeling I have that I can't seem to shake." He wrinkled his brow. "She never wants me to take her home. Do you know much about her or her family?"

"Not really."

"I think she likes me. And I like her, too.

It's just I feel like I'm missing something important about her."

Judith was coming to realize that she was feeling the same way about Ben. Though their conversations were fairly easy, and he was always courteous to her, she was sure he was keeping something from her. "I guess all you can do is try and talk to her," she mumbled.

Caleb's expression turned bleak. "I'll try.

"Good luck, brother. I best get in here before Mamm wonders why I'm taking my time."

"And she will," Caleb said with a laugh. "I'll go downstairs and try to distract her."

Judith went through her morning routine as quickly as possible, then raced downstairs. There she found Ben sitting at the table with Maggie. They both looked up at her when she approached the table with a bowl of hot oatmeal.

"Hi, Judith!" Maggie said before picking up a crayon and handing it to Ben. "Color the horse blue," she commanded to Ben.

"Maggie, don't speak that way to our guest."

"It's all right, Judith," Ben said. "We're just having fun together."

Having fun together? Since when did Ben enjoy sitting with a five-year-old and coloring? Pushing that question aside, she concentrated on her little sister's behavior. "Even if you two are only having fun, that's no way to talk to people, *shveshtah*."

Immediately, Maggie looked contrite. "I'm sorry."

Ben raised his eyes to Judith's before concentrating back on Maggie. "Why should the horse be blue? I thought Beauty was right fine as a brown horse."

"This ain't Beauty. She's outside in her stall."

"Ah. Yes, I suppose she is," he murmured. "So the ones in the book are blue?"

"Yup. I want pretty horses."

"Then that's what you should have," he said. Just as if it made perfect sense.

Though Judith had colored her share of pink, purple, and blue horses, she was still caught off guard seeing Ben in this new light. Somewhat stunned, she sat down.

The evidence was right there in front of her, as plain as day. He was now very different from the boy she'd known back in school. He wasn't trying to be shocking, he was trying to fit in. And he didn't get angry, not even when Anson asked him a hundred questions or her father asked him to work late . . . or Maggie told him to color the horses on her book correctly.

Her heart softened toward him just a little more—or maybe she just realized she was finally allowing herself to like him very much.

"Judith?" he said, looking at her curiously. "Are you all right?"

"Oh. *Jah.* Sure."

He smiled at her then and went back to coloring beside Maggie.

Judith leaned back and watched the two of them, just to see what he would do next.

Of course, what he did shouldn't have been a surprise. After picking out a crayon, he began to color the horse blue. Even going as far as to outline it as well.

Maggie got to her feet and braced her hands on his shoulders, before nodding. "You are doing *gut*. That's a pretty horse."

"Thank you, Maggie. What color should the grass be?"

Maggie giggled. "Green, of course."

"Of course." He picked up another crayon and got to work. Looking quietly content. As if there was nothing he'd rather be doing.

And as Judith watched, she knew the worst thing possible was happening. Little by little, her heart was becoming claimed by Ben Knox. It came as something of a surprise, too. Here, she'd gotten by for so long, planning and organizing, doing everything right. Weighing consequences.

But none of that seemed to matter. All that did matter was that when she looked at Ben, her insides warmed. And her pulse raced . . . and before she knew it, she was smiling at him.

And he was smiling right back at her.

Thirty minutes later, as they left the shelter of the barn, the bright day seemed blinding.

"When have you ever seen such a blue sky in December?" Ben asked, smiling as he guided Beauty down the snow-packed driveway.

"I'm sure I can't remember." Unable to keep the wistfulness from her voice, Judith said, "I thought we were due for more snow."

"The newspapers said tomorrow, I think."

"Maybe it will continue until Christmas

Day," she said, enchanted by the idea. "Wouldn't that be *wunderbaar*? To have a white Christmas? Then it would be the most perfect day imaginable."

He shrugged. "I suppose."

The sadness in his eyes couldn't be ignored. At least, not any longer. "Ben, why did you come back? Really?"

He said nothing as he guided the buggy onto the main street, then got Beauty settled, letting her clip-clop along, staying to the side of the traffic.

Feeling embarrassed, she rested her back against the lightly cushioned seat. "I'm sorry. I shouldn't have pried."

"It's not that I didn't want to answer you," he said slowly. "It's just that I don't know the right answer."

"You honestly don't know why you came back?"

He shook his head. "Not exactly. At first, it was to see Sugarcreek one last time. Then it was because I wanted to put the house up for sale. To end everything here."

"End?"

"You know what I mean. I needed to move on with my life. I still do."

"You weren't happy here, were you?"

"Honestly?"

"Of course."

"No. No, I wasn't happy here at all." His lips thinned, as if even remembering his hardships caused true pain.

She ached to understand. "Because your *mamm* was sick?"

"Oh, Judith. She wasn't sick. She left because she was unhappy."

Dismay that he'd gone through such a terrible situation—and that she'd been oblivious to it—almost stole her breath away. "And what of your *daed*? Did you get along with him?"

He shook his head. As they stopped at a light he looked at her again. "Judith, for most of my life, my parents didn't expect much from me. As far as I could tell, they saw me as more of a burden than anything. But I got used to that. What hurt was that no one challenged them. Ever."

"What do you mean?"

"Teachers. Friends of my parents. Even people like you . . . were determined to believe I was bad. No matter what I did, it seemed like I was only seen in a bad light. When I was late to school, the teacher was sure it was because I was lazy—never that I had to stay at home and finish my chores." As Beauty carried them forward, he clicked his tongue softly to the horse, then continued. "Later, when I failed a test, everyone always assumed it was because I didn't care about school. That I didn't try." He glanced her way. "No one ever thought that maybe I honestly didn't understand the material."

"I'm sorry."

He looked toward the horizon. "You shouldn't be. A lot of the time, I kept so many of my feelings hidden, most people were probably afraid to even try to help me. I'm not going to lie—I know a lot of the times I was a pretty bad kid."

"I never thought you were bad."

He clicked to Beauty again, encouraging her to pick up the pace. "Come now, Judith. You might not have told people I was bad . . . but you certainly didn't think that I was any good."

"I was nervous," she blurted. Appalled that she shared such news with him. And appalled that she still felt the same way. To some extent. "Being around you made me nervous."

"Why?"

"Because you didn't follow the rules. And even more, you seemed to find the rules amusing."

"That's because all those rules about proper behavior never seemed to apply to me."

"That's not true."

"Judith, I can't tell you the number of evenings I was denied supper because I wasn't good enough. Or the number of times it was suggested I should *not* attend a singing or a gathering because I might be disruptive. No one gave me a chance. No one ever wanted to take the chance that maybe, just maybe, they were wrong."

"Is that what you think about me? Ben, you don't have to believe me, but I never wanted to believe the worst in you. I'm not that horrible."

"You're not horrible at all, Judith." He turned the buggy into the store's parking lot, then neatly guided Beauty into the shelter at the back of the store. "I've never thought that. Besides. If anyone did have the right to think only the worst of me, it would have to be you."

She frowned. "What do you mean?"

After pulling up the brake, he reached for her hand. "I mean that I knew I made you uncomfortable. And that I don't blame your actions. Truth be told, there were a number of times when I tried to make nervous."

"Why?"

"Because to me, you were everything good. Because you had everything I knew I didn't have."

"Ben, you're making no sense . . ."

"Judith, when I looked at you, I saw your brothers who looked out for you. I saw your mother, who came up as often as she could to help out. I saw the way your *daed* smiled at you when we were at church, and I saw how the teacher praised your perfect grades. To me, you were perfect . . . and I knew I was far from that."

When she stared at him in shock, he shook his head in wonder. As if she was truly the silliest woman on the planet. "Because I've liked you for years, Judith Graber. You are everything a man wants. And everything a man dreams about."

"Me?" she sputtered.

"You. Judith, you are proper and lovely. You have a family that everyone admires.

You treat others well and are as smart as any man." Looking down at his hands, he continued, his voice barely above a whisper. "See, for as long as I can remember, I wished you were my girl."

She was confused and flattered and shocked and thrilled. But above all that, she ached for him. Ached that he'd been so misunderstood, by all of them. "I didn't know," she said softly. "I didn't know how you felt."

He dropped her hand and sat back. "Now you do. Now you know yet another reason why I came back." He tucked his chin, like he was embarrassed for her to know. "I wanted to see you one last time."

Though his confessions were spinning in her mind, she couldn't quite bring all the strands together. "I'm sorry. I still don't know . . ."

He opened his door and hopped out. "Don't worry," he said as he helped her down and then unfastened the leads around Beauty. "I know nothing will come of it. I know you would never feel the same."

Her face was so heated, her emotions in such turmoil . . . Judith scurried past him and unlocked the door. Flicking switches, she turned up the heat and the lights as she walked toward the front of the store. As the scent of cinnamon and peppermint wafted through the air and a hint of orange gingerbread tickled her senses, Judith sorted through everything she'd just heard.

Tried to catch her breath.

And realized, right there and then, that Benjamin Knox might be right about a lot of things, but he was terribly wrong, too.

Though some people might never ever like him, she was not one of those people.

And really never had been.

What was true then was true now.

She still liked him very much.

But how could she ever tell him?

Chapter Fourteen

Four Days Until Christmas

"Rebecca, there's one last basket to deliver," Caleb announced as they entered the back of his family's store. Judith had told them the baskets could be held in the refrigerated section for as long as needed, but now it was time to finish passing them out. In another hour it would be getting dark. And though it wasn't snowing, the clouds were foreboding enough to signal that snow was on the way. He didn't want to worry about Rebecca getting home safely.

As Becca walked toward him—she'd

gone inside the store to say hello to his sister—her eyes lit up. “Only one basket left? Thank goodness. With each delivery, the baskets felt like they grew in size. My arms are getting tired.”

“I bet.” Each one truly had seemed a little heavier than the last. Thinking of their last delivery, he wiped a hand over her brow. “I thought I was never going to get to put Mrs. Schrock’s basket down.”

Rebecca giggled. “It did look doubtful. She had you holding it for a good fifteen minutes while she picked the perfect spot.”

With each passing minute the filled basket had felt like it had gained a load of bricks. “My arms were groaning so much, I was tempted to drop it onto the floor and walk away.”

“But you didn’t.”

“I was closer than you think.”

She giggled. “At least it’s all over now. I’ll take care of this one, Caleb.”

“Of course you won’t.” Now side by side in the cool room, he playfully flexed his arms. “We’re in this together, you know. I would never let you deliver it without me. Who does it go to?”

"Oh, no one you know."

Surprised, he turned to her. There was something new in her voice. Hesitation? Worry? "Why wouldn't I know this family?" he asked, scanning her face for clues.

"They don't get out too much."

"But still, I'm sure I know them. I've known everyone else."

"It's just . . ." her cheeks bloomed. "This family is pretty proud. I think it would be better if I delivered it. By myself. Just so they don't get embarrassed."

Now he was a little bit offended. "I can keep a secret, Becca."

"I know you can." She turned away, fussed with one of the towels folded in the basket.

But she obviously didn't. "Rebecca, you don't think I would go tell people about these needy families, do ya? Or worse, talk about them? Because I wouldn't." Did she honestly think he would be so cruel? "I'm happy to help others. I'm not looking to make myself feel better by comparing their circumstances. I'm not like that."

She bit her lip, looking more and more troubled. "Caleb, don't worry so. It's just, well . . . you've done enough. I'll take care of this one. It would be best."

To his amazement, she walked right in front of him and reached out for the basket. Just as if she carried heavy things down all over Sugarcreek all the time.

Not even thinking, he stepped in front of her, blocking her way. "No."

She stilled. "No?"

"Rebecca, no way am I going to let you do that. These baskets are heavy. I'd say they're easily over fifty pounds." Because that didn't sound all that heavy, he added, "At least sixty pounds. They might even be closer to seventy. Or even more. They're way too heavy for you to carry. You could hurt yourself."

Once again, she stepped to the side. "I'll be okay."

"No you won't. Even if they weren't so heavy, it's going to be dark out soon."

She sighed. "Caleb—"

"Rebecca." Though he was acting childish, he darted in front of her and clasped the basket tight. His sore muscles strained a bit as he held it up. "I've started this project with you, and I'm going to see it through. Let's go."

"Caleb . . ."

"Open the door for me so I can put this in the back of the buggy," he ordered. He didn't like to speak to her in such a harsh tone of voice, but his frustration with her stubborn nature was getting the best of him. He was trying to look out for her. Help her. Didn't she see that?

After another incredibly long minute, Rebecca did as he bid, then helped him get the basket secure in the back of his courting buggy.

Though he knew he probably shouldn't feel so full of himself, he puffed up with masculine pride. Finally, he was getting what he wanted: the chance to take care of her. To help her. Maybe even for always. "Do you have all of your things? Because I intend to take you home afterward."

He paused, half waiting for her to fight him again.

But instead of doing that, she climbed into the buggy seat. *"Jah."*

He could tell she was upset. Caleb thought about apologizing, but in a flash, he recalled all the times he'd watched his older brother Joshua taking care of Gretta. Without fail, he'd helped her into the buggy, or fetched her things when she'd been as big as a house at the end of her pregnancy.

Now, even when they came back home for a visit, Joshua waited on his wife, getting Gretta a cup of tea, or encouraging her to lie down when it was obvious to one and all that baby Will had tired out his mother.

Everyone in the family had smiled at the sight of Josh fussing with cups and saucers, but inside, Caleb knew the entire family was proud of the man the oldest Graber had become.

And that—for better or worse—was how Caleb wanted to be. He wanted to be a man Rebecca could depend on, no matter what. Not just for lifting heavy baskets, but for dealing with heavy issues, too.

After folding a thick wool blanket around both their laps, he said, "Where to?"

"Down the street. Then turn on Fourth."

"All right." With a click, he motioned Star forward, out of the covering and into the sunlight.

They turned right, then with a click of the reins, Star picked up her pace. Along she went, head high, seeming eager to prance among the festive decorations strung along the hills of Main Street. Star's quick, steady gait kept a breeze blowing around them, chafing his cheeks and ears.

"Are you cold?"

Rebecca shrugged. "Only a little."

"Why don't you scoot a little closer? You'd be warmer."

After a second's hesitation, she took his advice and moved next to him. The moment they made contact, her body heat mixed with his.

When they came to Fourth Street, he turned right. "Where to now?"

"At the stop sign, turn left."

Caleb nodded, worried about her. She sounded so sad. Like she was on her way to a funeral or something. And after he turned left, he slowed Star a bit. "And now?"

"In three blocks, turn right. The house is the first on the left."

"All right." Looking around, Caleb felt so proud of himself for volunteering to help Rebecca. Here in this part of Sugarcreek, most of the houses were very small, some in disrepair.

A couple of the houses were owned by *Englischers*—there were old cars in the driveways. A couple other houses looked Amish; they were dark and void of decorations.

However, cloaking it all was the prevailing feeling of need and want.

Those were foreign feelings. He'd never gone hungry; it was pretty much an impossibility when your family owned a store, he supposed.

He hated the idea of someone having nothing to eat in the middle of the winter like this. Especially during the blessed Christmas season.

And though they hadn't delivered a basket to a person who hadn't been gracious and thankful, the truth was, he didn't feel great about Rebecca visiting one of these houses alone. Even the Amish weren't always polite. Even some of their community could be harsh or grumpy or had tempers . . .

Some might not be suitable company for someone as sweet and kind as Rebecca Yoder.

At last, he pulled to a stop in front of a terribly rundown house. Paint was peeling off the siding, old shades showed through the windows. But more than that, there was such a sense of depression mixed with desperation about the place, that it felt almost contagious.

That feeling, mixed with Rebecca's withdrawn attitude, finally made sense. This place made her nervous.

Well, he could understand that. The place looked so neglected, it stood to reason that whoever lived there might feel hopeless enough to be dangerous. Especially to a sweet woman like Becca.

Since he was especially eager to do whatever it took to make her happy, he decided to take charge.

"Here we are," he said with more than a solid helping of false brightness. "How about you just wait here while I go deliver this? It won't take long, and you can stay warm." Though they'd delivered the other baskets together, he didn't think she'd mind skipping out on this one.

But instead of looking relieved, Rebecca's eyes turned teary.

"Don't worry, I'll tell them this basket is your doing . . ." he said softly, though he didn't know why he said such a thing. Never once had she acted like she needed to hear praise for her actions. "They'll understand you needing to stay here under the blanket."

"Stop," she blurted.

"Stop?" He turned to her. Twin tears traipsed down her cheeks. Breaking his heart. "Becca, sweetheart . . . What is wrong?" As he heard his words, he felt himself blush. For sure she had to be shocked that he uttered such an endearment.

But if anything, the tears only fell a little faster.

Unable to stop himself, he brushed a tear away with the side of his thumb. Her eyes closed, and he could have sworn he heard her sigh. "Becca?"

Just as she opened her mouth, the front door of the house opened and a woman came out. "Rebecca? What are you doing just sitting out here?" Crossing her arms over her chest, she looked at Caleb and frowned. "And who are you?"

As he sat beside her, stunned, Rebecca scrambled off of the seat. "Nothing, Mamm."

Mamm? This was her mother? This was her house?

Though he was shocked as could be, he darted out and approached her mother. "Hi, Mrs. Yoder. I'm Caleb Graber."

"And I'm Mrs. Yoder. Rebecca's mother, of course." With a soft smile at Rebecca, who still hadn't joined them, Mrs. Yoder said, "Rebecca has told me that she's been spending a lot of time with you—I wondered when you were going to take the time to visit her here."

Rebecca's cheeks burned bright. "Mamm, don't."

Pushing aside his excuses—the almost overwhelming need to assure Mrs. Yoder that he had tried to come calling at her home—Caleb spoke quickly. "*Jah.* I've been helping her with the Christmas baskets," he said. Then, seeing the pained expression on Rebecca's face, wished he could have cut his tongue out. "I mean, I like being with Rebecca."

Mrs. Yoder smiled distractedly, now looking at the big basket in the back of his buggy. "Is that one of them?"

Looking at Rebecca, who still wouldn't meet his gaze, Caleb nodded. "It is. And it just happens to be for your family."

"Really? My goodness, that's a beautiful basket."

"Everyone has seemed to really like them," he said, walking to the back of the buggy. "I'll bring this one inside for you."

"Nee," Rebecca blurted. "I'll take care of it."

Though he knew this moment was paining her, that she was embarrassed, Caleb instinctively knew that if he stepped away now, he might never get her back. "I am going to carry this for you," he said gently. "I am going to carry this inside your home."

Looking miserable, she walked to her mother, who led them inside.

Arms full of basket, Caleb followed as best as he could, taking care not to trip on the single step leading into the house.

Inside, the house looked as rundown as the outside. The furniture was scarred and marked. It was dark and quiet. And cool. Almost cold.

Ten steps later, he arrived in the kitchen. With relief, he set the basket down.

"Caleb. *Danke.* It was good of you to help Rebecca bring this here."

"I wanted to," he said with a smile, just as Amanda, Rebecca's younger sister, appeared out of a back room. "Hi, Mandy."

Amanda, three years younger than Rebecca but so very far from her older sister in temperament, grinned his way. "Hi, Caleb," she said, then stared at the basket in wonder. "What's this?"

"Rebecca and I have been delivering Christmas baskets. Because we helped, we each get one. I'm just helping her get hers home."

Fingering the wicker, Mrs. Yoder glanced his way. "Indeed? You got one, too?"

"For sure," he lied. Though he knew he shouldn't be telling such tales, he was eager to do anything to make Rebecca feel less self-conscious.

Mandy circled the basket like a curious bird, her fingers darting and pointing at the contents. "Mamm, look! There're towels and braided bread. And cookies!"

Mandy's enthusiasm made Caleb grin. But if anything, Rebecca looked even paler. In addition, she seemed to be refusing to meet his gaze. Her head was tilted toward the floor, shame emanating in sharp waves.

Making her uncomfortable was the last thing he wanted.

"I should probably go," he said. "Mrs. Yoder, could I speak to Rebecca for a few moments?"

"Of course." With a tender look in her daughter's direction, she slipped her arm around Mandy's shoulders. "Becca, you go into the front room with your young man. Amanda and I will stay here and have some tea."

Amanda groaned.

With a wink Caleb's way, Mrs. Yoder said firmly, "And perhaps we'll try out some of these cookies in the basket."

Rebecca glanced at Caleb again, then led the way to the front room.

He followed, and kept following her until she stopped in the far corner of the room. Next to a fireplace that looked like it hadn't been used in weeks.

When she stopped and then finally faced him again, there was such a defeated look in her expression that it took his breath away. Just like she'd lost a race that she should have won.

He stayed quiet. Waiting. Clenched his

fists so he wouldn't be tempted to reach out for her. Rebecca was obviously struggling to keep ahold of her pride.

Finally she spoke. "I'm sorry. I am so very sorry," she whispered.

"Sorry for what?"

"For lying to you."

He couldn't stop himself any longer. Giving in to temptation, he reached for her hands and tugged her closer. Her hands were stiff and cold in his own, but at least she wasn't pulling away. Brushing his thumbs against her knuckles, he warmed her soft skin. "You didn't lie to me."

"Caleb, I didn't tell you that while we were doing all these things for the poor, for the needy . . . I was one of them."

"If I look upset, it's because I hate the idea of you going without." *Especially without food,* he silently added.

"I never wanted you to see this."

"I don't care where you live, Rebecca."

"I do."

"Is this why you never let me walk you home or drive here to pick you up?"

She nodded.

"Well, now I know." Rubbing his thumb over her knuckles again, he murmured,

"So, Becca, now will you let me pick you up?"

"I . . . I can't see you no more."

He was stunned. "What? Why?"

"Caleb. You know why."

He knew she was embarrassed. But he also realized he wasn't going to let her focus on her embarrassment. There was too much between them to give up because of pride or a silly misunderstanding. "Is it because I lied to your *mamm* about how we got the baskets?" He released her hands, ready to make things right. "If that's it, I'll go tell her the truth."

"Nee!" Tears filled her eyes. "Caleb, I wanted you to think we were equals. But that was wrong of me, because I knew we were too different. Now things can't be fixed."

"I don't care how much money your family has or where you live. All I care about is you. I only want to be with you."

Rebecca turned away. Lowering her voice, she said, "My *daed* got laid off from work last year. He tried to find a job, but he has a bad arm, so no one would hire him. He finally found work, but it's in Toledo. So the extra money he's making has to go for his living expenses."

"I understand." Looking at the empty fireplace, he started realizing all the things she was doing without, the many things he'd been taking for granted. "Tomorrow, I'm going to bring you some wood so you can have a fire."

"Caleb, please do not. I don't want anything from you."

"All I would do is chop some from our woods and bring it over. It won't cost me anything."

"Please don't. Just go."

"But Rebecca, I want to be with you." He paused, then rushed forward, stating the obvious. "I like you a lot, you know."

Her expression remained skeptical. "I know you're just being kind."

"I'm not." All at once, he wanted to tell her that he loved her. That he was willing to do whatever he needed to do to make sure she was warm and comfortable.

Because, well, he fully intended to marry her one day.

But how do you tell a girl that? Especially at a moment like this?

"Please go."

He stepped backward, giving her room. "When can I see you again?"

"I don't know. We've delivered the baskets. There's no reason to see each other now."

"Sure there is."

She walked to the door and opened it. Wide. "Please, Caleb," she said softly.

He did as she asked. Because she was hurting. Because he didn't want to make her more upset.

But leaving her like this wasn't right.

"I'm going to see you soon," he said as he stepped through the threshold. "And you and your family are coming to our house for Christmas dinner."

"All three of us?"

"Of course. And you better make it sound like the best invitation you've ever received, Becca Yoder, or I'll do the asking. I want to be with you on Christmas Day."

"Why?"

Because he knew they were meant to be together. Because he was going to tell her his true feelings for her—as soon as the time was right.

But all that felt too pushy. "Because I have a gift for you," he said instead.

But yet again, that was the wrong thing.

Panic lit her eyes. “Oh, Caleb—”

“Shh. I didn’t spend any money.”

“But I don’t have a gift for you.”

“Then let your gift for me be your company.” That would be the best gift, anyway.

Reaching for her hands again, he said, “Rebecca, please just say you will. If for no other reason, for Amanda and for your *mamm*. You know they’ll enjoy being with my family.”

“All right.” She squeezed his hands, though she still looked doubtful.

“You made me happy, Rebecca. *Danke.*”

And with that, he turned around. Feeling that he’d aged ten years in the last hour. And, perhaps, just gotten the most wonderful gift in the world—honesty between them. And the promise of a future.

Chapter Fifteen

Three Days Until Christmas

Lilly felt bad about lying to Robert, but if she had told him she was going to Berlin, he would have asked her a bunch of questions. And then she would have felt guilty. So she'd told him she was going to her mother's house, helping with Carrie for a bit so her mother could do some shopping.

As soon as she got to Berlin, she drove directly to a jewelry store she'd seen an ad for in the Sunday paper. After getting a close parking place, she entered the quiet store and smiled at the woman standing behind a counter decorated with bright gold garlands.

"How may I help you?"

"I'm looking for a watch. For my husband."

The lady blinked, then looked her up and down a little more closely. "You seem awfully young to be married."

Lilly tried not to shy away under the clerk's scrutiny. "Would you be able to help me?"

"Of course." The lady's perfect hairdo hardly moved as she came out from behind the counter and directed Lilly to another glass case. "What kind of watch? Digital? Quartz? Silver? Stainless steel?"

The choices seemed endless. "I'm not sure."

"That's fair. How about we start looking at them?"

One by one, the sales associate took out the watches. Accordingly, Lilly lifted them up, examined the faces. Tried to imagine whether Robert would want something traditional or high tech.

The digital watch with the black rubber band didn't seem right. "I think my husband needs something more traditional."

Instantly, the digital watches went away. "What about these?" the sales clerk asked. "They're stainless, easy to read, and have a lifetime warranty."

"Lifetime?"

"You heard that right," the lady said with pride. "If anything happens to the watch or the band, just bring it back here and we'll fix it or replace it for free."

Lilly took hold of the stainless-steel watch. The metal was cool in her hands while its weight felt substantial. As she gazed at it, she tried to imagine it on Robert's wrist. "It's pretty," she said. "I like the silver links. They seem sturdy."

"Oh, they are," the lady said, leaning her elbows on the top of the glass case. "That brand is my favorite, too. The watches look simple, but they're good quality. You know, that watch will be something that a man would be proud to pass on to his children."

To be passed on to their children. That had a nice ring to it, she thought. "And he could bring this in to get fixed even next year?"

"Dear, your son could bring it in to get fixed. Lifetime means lifetime of the watch."

Lilly couldn't help but smile at the thought of giving something so special to Robert that he could pass it on to their children. "My husband, he's been wearing his grandfather's pocket watch. It just broke, and he's at loose ends."

"I promise, he'll enjoy this. It's a fantastic present. Something you'll be proud to give him."

Lilly could only imagine how great it would be to see a complete look of contentment and pleasure on Robert's face when he opened her gift. "How much is it?"

The woman slipped on her reading glasses. "Three hundred dollars."

Lilly was so taken aback, she almost dropped the watch on the glass countertop. "Three hundred?"

Slowly, the woman reclaimed the watch. "Why yes, dear. You saw the brand. This is a very nice timepiece. Quality."

"I'm afraid I can't afford it."

"What can you afford?"

"Under a hundred dollars." It took everything she had to keep her expression even. An hour before, the amount sounded respectable. Now, though, it sounded completely inappropriate.

"I can still help you. Don't worry." She reached into the cabinet, quickly put away the expensive watch, and pulled out another tray. "These are all nice. Maybe one of them will fit your needs?"

Lilly picked up several and examined them. They were fine.

But compared to the one she'd been holding with the lifetime warranty, they seemed like poor copies of better things.

"Do any of them catch your interest?"

"Not as much. I'm afraid I'm going to have to think about things."

"Well, don't think for too long! It is the twenty-third, you know."

"Are you open tomorrow?" Maybe she could run over in the early afternoon? If she got up and baked at dawn . . .

"Only until noon."

Her heart sank. "Not later?"

"I'm sorry, dear. But I'm anxious to be with my family. Christmas comes but once a year, you know."

"Yes. Of course." Making herself step away, she smiled weakly. "Thanks for showing me the watches."

"You're welcome." Sympathy showed on her face when she continued. "Maybe you could open an account? Then you could charge the gift?"

"No. I couldn't do that." Even if she had a credit history, she didn't want to do something like that without Robert's permission.

"Merry Christmas."

"Yes. Merry Christmas," she said as she left. After getting into her car, she hesitated. The lady's words about it being the twenty-third really hit home. It was time to do something or she would have nothing. And the thought of not having anything to give Robert on Christmas morning was a terrible one.

Looking at her laptop, Lilly considered trying to find another jewelry store nearby. Maybe someplace else would have a better deal?

Not that it really mattered. She knew what she wanted. She just couldn't afford it.

When her stomach growled, she decided to run into a tiny diner and grab a bowl of soup.

After getting a piping hot bowl of vegetable soup, she sat at the counter and halfheartedly glanced at a flyer that someone had left behind.

The flyer was filled with ads for after-

Christmas sales, which made her smile. It seemed no matter what the season, everyone was anxious to rush it.

Then, there on the bottom of the second page, was the answer to her prayers. "We buy computers."

Slowly, she put her spoon down. Was she really willing to do that? Was she willing to sell her laptop in order to buy Robert something of value?

It seemed like a horrible idea. She absolutely loved her laptop. She wrote a journal, kept up with friends, read the news, even listened to music on it. For the last year, it had been her link to the outside world, especially those first few months in Sugarcreek, when she'd felt so lonely and confused.

But Robert seemed to be wary of it. Actually, he teased her about "playing" on it at least once a day.

Maybe he felt she was too obsessed with it? After all, before he left the Amish he'd never had electricity, and certainly never needed a computer.

Though he'd gained some new freedoms, and even seemed to enjoy many of the conveniences he now had in his life, he'd also sacrificed his relationship with his family. And though he never complained too much about it, she knew the strained relationship weighed on him.

What she needed to do was not just tell him that she loved him, but show him, too. If she sold the computer, that sacrifice would mean something to him, wouldn't it? It would show him how much she loved him . . .

"Need anything else, hon?"

Before she lost her nerve, Lilly pushed the flyer toward the waitress. "Do you know if this place is nearby?"

After scanning the ad, she nodded. "It's just around the corner."

"Do you know anything about it?" Half of her hoped the woman was going to tell her it was dangerous. Not reputable.

"My cousin-in-law owns it," she said proudly. "They're good people there. Whatcha trying to sell?"

"My laptop."

"If it's in good condition, I'll bet they'll snap it up. Lots of people on hard times who need a computer for a good price, you know."

Making her decision, Lilly got to her feet.

"I'll go over there now. How much do I owe you for the soup?"

The lady looked her over, then shook her head and smiled. "Not a thing."

"But—"

"Consider it my treat. A Christmas treat. You seem like a real sweet girl, and it's just a bowl of soup."

"Thanks. And Merry Christmas!" After smiling at the waitress again, Lilly grabbed the flyer and went back to her car. Ready to finally do something Robert would be proud of. Ready to give him something she knew without a doubt he would value.

Chapter Sixteen

Christmas Eve

The store had been almost empty all day, making Judith even more aware of Ben—and that their time together was almost over. Though there seemed to be a new understanding between them, there was also a new tension.

There had also been very little time to talk privately. Both her father and Joshua had been in the store all day, taking inventory and organizing merchandise for when they would open on the twenty-sixth.

For the last hour, she'd been at the counter. Standing and waiting on the occasional customer while Ben had been asked to do lots of heavy lifting.

Every time he walked by her, Ben glanced her way but never stopped to talk. Or flirt. Which was what he used to be intent on doing when they'd been alone.

"Judith, time to close up shop," her father announced. "It's three o'clock."

Since the store was empty anyway, she walked to the door and dutifully turned the sign. "What would you like me to do now?"

"Go with Ben to his house, then meet us later at home."

Judith scanned the area for Ben. When she met his gaze, she raised a brow. He shook his head and shrugged.

Letting her know that this was news to him as well.

"All right," she said slowly. "Ben? Are you ready?"

"I am. I'll meet you at the buggy."

"You okay?" Joshua asked as he approached her side. "You look a little worried."

After seeing that their father was out of

earshot, she shrugged. Almost mimicking the same gesture Ben had done. "I'm not sure what is going on."

"Daed's trying to matchmake, of course."

"With me and Ben?"

"Of course." A slow smile lit his face. "Who else would he be concentrating on?"

"That's embarrassing. Joshua, is Daed really worried that I can't find a man on my own?"

Crossing his arms over his chest, Joshua shook his head. "That's not why our father is trying to get in the middle of things."

"Why is he, then?"

"For an obvious reason. Judith, all of us can see that there's something pretty special between you two."

"There might be. I'm not sure . . ."

"You're still not sure? What's wrong?"

"Back in school, I was a little afraid of him," she confided.

"We all were, at least a little bit," Joshua agreed. "But though he and I weren't good friends, I discovered that a lot of people never gave him a chance. But now that I've gotten to know him better, I have to say that he seems like a good man."

Privately, she agreed. With every hour

that passed, he took each perception of hers and turned it, allowing her to see him in a new way. “He had a difficult home life.”

“I heard that, too.” A faraway look entered his eyes, and Judith wondered if he was thinking about Gretta. She, too, had had some challenges at home. “We can’t help how we grow up, Judith. All we can do is grow up and move on.”

Feeling comforted by her brother’s pronouncement, and remembering the heartfelt discussions they’d shared when Josh had been falling in love, she decided to open up more. “Ben makes me feel things I didn’t know I could feel—at least any longer. When I’m with Ben, I feel like I’m five years old again and getting ready to go to McDonald’s. Around him, I’m nervous and excited all at the same time.”

She tensed, half ready for her older brother to tease her. She wouldn’t blame him if he did. What she was saying was terribly revealing. She wasn’t used to opening herself up to ridicule.

But instead of belittling her, he squeezed her shoulder. “Don’t take this the wrong way, but I think you should stop overthinking so much.”

"Around Ben or about my feelings?"

"About it all."

"You never acted like this around Gretta, did you?"

Joshua gaped at her before speaking. "Wow, Judith. You really weren't paying me much attention last winter were you?"

"I was."

"I was completely twisted up and confused with Gretta. She made me crazy! I could hardly stop thinking about her. And when she went riding with Roland? I could have spit nails."

"Spit nails?" She raised a brow.

He waved a hand at her superior air. "I'm not sayin' Ben is your future, but he's a good man. And it's obvious he cares about you. Enjoy being cared for."

But she had Ben issues. Mixed up in the present was their past. There were too many memories of him being difficult and angry to let her forget it all.

"Judith?" their father called out. "Are you ever going to listen the first time? Please leave, daughter."

Listen the first time? "Daed, I'm not a—"

"Don't say it," Joshua interrupted.

"What, daughter?"

"And don't bother arguing," Joshua said under his breath. "Just listen and go."

"Judith?" her father called out.

"Nothing, father. I'm coming now." She started walking forward. "Joshua, when did you get so smart?" she asked over her shoulder.

"I've always been smart. You just never listened before."

She was still chuckling about her brother's parting comment when she got to the shed. Ben was standing beside Beauty, rubbing her neck as he waited for her.

Judith quickened her step. "I'm sorry I kept you waiting. I started talking to Joshua."

"It was no problem. You ready now?"

When she nodded, he helped her into the buggy, then slid in beside her. As their bodies touched, Judith realized that she no longer sat beside him so stiffly. Instead, she was becoming used to him. Very used to him.

But what did that mean?

"Why are we going to your house?"

He cleared his throat. "Your parents invited me to spend the night."

"For Christmas Eve and Christmas Day?"

He winced. "Yes," he said slowly. "I take it you didn't know about this?"

"Nee."

"Are you upset?"

"No," she said quickly, though she wasn't sure if she was lying or not. "Just surprised." Scanning his face, she waited for a reaction. But instead of saying something in return he seemed to retreat into himself.

Now she felt terrible. She'd been surprised because they never had entertained guests for Christmas before. With their large family, there'd never been the need. Or maybe just never the room?

"We're here," he said quietly. "Would you like to stay here while I go in?"

"I'd like to come with you, if I may."

Without another word, he slid out of his side then walked toward the modest two-story house. The siding was whitewashed. Four blue spruce pine trees ran along the side of the property. Now, with fluffy pristine snowflakes decorating the boughs, the trees looked like English Christmas trees.

But what really caught her attention was

the blue and white realty sign standing proudly in the middle of the lawn.

Ben didn't spare any of it a look as he walked up the driveway along the short pathway to the front porch and up the steps. Without taking out keys, he opened the door and walked inside.

Only then did he look her way. "Judith?"

"Oh. Yes. I'm sorry." Gosh, here she was, apologizing again. "I was looking at your pine trees. They're really pretty, all covered with snow." There was no way she was going to tell him that the sign in his yard made her sad.

"Ah."

She noticed he still didn't spare the trees a look.

Once inside, she was besieged by the musky smell of a house largely unused. Though everything was fairly clean—the furniture looked recently dusted and the floor was swept—it felt completely empty.

Empty in a way that had nothing to do with lack of furniture and children's coats and Toby toys and her mother's baking or her siblings' noise.

It was empty from lack of use.

Judith hadn't failed to notice that he left

the door open and seemed oddly reluctant to even step much farther into the home.

"This isn't a happy place for you, is it?"

Ben started. Then, with a look of resignation, he shook his head. "As I told you before, my *muddah* left when I was thirteen. When she left, everything changed." He paused, then added, "Not that things were any good before."

The cold air wafting through the open door was making her chilled. Instead of closing the door, she moved toward the kitchen. Again, the room was spotless but extremely empty. Running a finger along the beige laminate, she turned to him. "Did your *mamm* ever say why she left? Did your *daed* ever talk to you about his feelings?"

His laugh was bitter. "Judith, my father was not one for letting us in. And as for my *mamm,* well I never heard from her again."

She couldn't imagine either of her parents acting so harsh. She couldn't imagine leaving her children, either. "She didn't contact you? She didn't write you letters and try to explain? Ever?"

"That's what I just said."

"What did your *daed* say?"

"He never spoke of it." He rolled his eyes. "Just one day she was gone."

She felt his despair like a tangible thing and wished she could do something to make his past easier to bear. It made her want to cry. "What did you do?"

The cloudy look that had filled his expression vanished as a new sardonic one took over. "What do think I did? I went to school the next day."

"And your sister? What did she do?" she asked, hoping for Ben to relieve her imagination. All she could think about at the moment was a too-young Ben being alone with no one to confide in.

"Beth is three years older. At first she stayed and helped with the house—Daed didn't give her much choice. But when she turned eighteen, she moved to my aunt's and eventually married an *Englischer*."

"Do you keep in touch with her? Do you see her often?"

But instead of answering he took off his hat and ran one hand through his hair. "Why all the questions, Judith? Why do you even care?"

It was on the tip of her tongue to tell him she didn't know. But she did.

And she acknowledged to herself that if he was brave enough to show her this very sad, empty house. If he was brave enough to share with her the pain of his mother's abandonment, then it was time for her to be honest.

"I'm asking because I care about you."

"What?"

"You heard me." She stepped closer to him. As she did so, Judith noticed the muscles tense under the cotton of his shirt. Almost like he was shielding himself from his reaction to her.

"I heard you but I don't understand you."

Her heart aching for all he'd lost, and for all he didn't believe he was worth, made her finally reveal what was in her heart. Even if they weren't destined to share a future, she wanted him to know that there was someone in his life who cared. "I think you do. I care about you. I like you and I want to know you better."

Ben blinked. "Why are you telling me this? Is it pity?"

"No."

"Why then?"

His voice was harsh, his expression shuttered. But while his voice, when it was like that, used to make her fearful, now she knew better. In his own way, Ben Knox was as scared as she was.

"Because I think you should know how I feel," she finally said. Realizing that deep in her heart, she wanted Ben to know that he was not alone. That even if nothing became of them, if there never was a romance, at the very least they now had a bond. "I didn't want you to leave Sugarcreek without knowing how I felt."

For a few seconds, his gaze softened. His eyes caressed her, like he wanted to memorize everything about this moment.

This wonderful, terrible, very, very sweet moment. "Even if I know." He cleared his throat. "Even if I felt that way, too . . . There's nothing we can do about it."

Even if he felt the same way. It took everything she had not to smile. "That's all right."

"It's all right? How can you say—" He cut himself off, obviously tongue-tied.

She smiled. "I'm not expectin' a marriage proposal." Though it pained her, she tried to smile. "I know you have plans. I don't want to mess them up."

Oh, right. His big plans. He had plans,

Ben thought bitterly to himself. Great plans. After Christmas, he was going to leave his house on the market and travel. Get on a bus, then a train, and go somewhere.

Get as far away from his memories as he possibly could.

"My things are in my bedroom. I'll be back."

A flash of pain registered in her eyes. And in response, Ben knew he'd upset her. He didn't understand the female mind all that well; most of the women he'd known hadn't thought enough of him to stick around. But even he knew he'd hurt her.

But what could he say?

He wasn't worth much.

He especially wasn't worth enough for Judith Graber to care about.

Keeping his back to her, he walked to his room and pulled out an extra set of clothes, his hairbrush and toothbrush. And then he pulled out the two Christmas gifts he'd bought for Maggie and Judith.

As he stared at the presents, wrapped up in bright foil-covered wrapping paper, he realized that no good would come from spending more time together. Especially not at her house. He liked her family too much, liked the sense of belonging too much. Because things between them were so tense . . . so raw . . . he had the feeling if he let down his guard even for a moment, he was going to start laying out his whole heart to her.

He'd do something stupid and tell her he loved her. Then, he'd begin to make plans. Before he knew it, it was likely he'd be talking about futures and marriage and children.

All things he didn't know a thing about.

And knowing him and his track record, he'd probably end up hurting her something awful. The way his parents had hurt each other.

Yes, it was far better to push her away now. For her own good.

Holding the packages, he left the duffle on his bed and returned to her with only the presents grasped in his hands instead.

When she saw his hands, a line formed between her brows. "Where's your bag?"

"It's in my room. You know, I was thinking that there's really no reason for me to come to your house. I'm going to stay here."

"You can't do that."

"Sure I can." He pushed the presents at her. Making sure to keep his voice level and even, he said, "Give the big one to Maggie, will you?"

She took them but looked troubled. "You need to give the gift to her yourself. You know how much Maggie likes you."

"I like her, too. But she'll understand why I can't be there."

"How could she? I don't."

"Judith, Christmas is a time for family."

"I know! That is why—"

Before she said something she'd regret, he said the obvious. "So I shouldn't be with yours. I'm not a Graber."

"That doesn't matter."

"It does to me. It would be awkward, being there."

"It won't. My parents invited you because they want you there."

Ignoring her protest, he continued. "I'd only be pretendin' that I belong when I don't. It will be better to be here."

"Here? Alone?"

She sounded so appalled, he almost smiled. "There's nothing wrong with that. Christmas is just a day."

"It's more than that."

Remembering all the days when he'd hoped it would mean more, he shook his head. "It doesn't have to be. Judith, I don't belong at your house tomorrow. It will be awkward."

"But . . . you don't have any other—"

Place to go, he finished silently. He stopped her before they could both hear the awful truth. "I know. But I'm okay with that." With effort, he tried to bring back his old harsh way of speaking. "Judith, the truth is that being around all of your family, it would make me really uncomfortable."

"We wouldn't . . ."

He interrupted her. "Sure you would. I've been on my own for a really long time now. I don't mind being alone. Please tell your parents thank you for me but I'll pass."

"I'm sorry. I shouldn't have said what I did."

"You shouldn't have told me that you care about me?" Ben grinned, just as if he could have cared less about her feelings. Or his, for that matter. "I care about you, too, *jah*? We've become friends, right?"

"Right." After a pause, she lifted the other present. "Who is this one for?"

"You."

She bit her lip. "Ben, please come with me."

"I'd rather not."

"May I open the present now?"

"No."

Seeing the hurt that flashed in her eyes, he gentled his tone. "I mean, it would be better to wait. It's not Christmas yet." To save them both a lot more embarrassment, he walked to the door.

Of course it was still open. He hated closing it. Had hated for her to be stuck inside this empty house filled with terrible memories even more. "Please go."

She stepped forward. Doubt and worry obvious in every step. "Ben—"

Before he could stop himself, he placed two fingers on her lips. "Please, Judith, don't say another word," he said softly.

When she stared back at him with wide eyes, he dropped his hand. "I promise you, it really is better this way. For both you and me. If I went to your house tonight, if I was there with everyone tomorrow, it would be too hard. Too painful. I'd rather not go at all."

For the first time in their acquaintance, Judith listened to him. She nodded, then turned around and walked to the buggy.

Ben stood away from the doorway so she wouldn't know he was watching. But he couldn't stop himself from watching her carefully open the door to the buggy, place the presents on the seat beside her, then click Beauty's reins.

Mere seconds later, she was gone.

"Merry Christmas," he said out of the open doorway.

Then he closed himself inside, shutting out the opportunity to actually be happy.

He felt as if the consequences of his actions were burning him deep. And he felt more of a failure than ever before. Though he'd grown up and had learned to control his anger and foster patience, he was still in many ways just a coward. It was still easier for him to be alone than to risk getting his feelings hurt. It was easier to shut himself off instead of waiting to have someone else shut him off first.

As he walked into the kitchen and spied the stack of library books on the counter, for once, they didn't bring him joy. All they did was remind him that it was far easier for him to read about other peoples' lives than to live fully and fearlessly.

Though he thought he'd changed a lot, it was becoming terribly apparent that he hadn't really changed at all.

Chapter Seventeen

Christmas Eve

"Caleb, what are you doing here?" Rebecca said from the other side of her half-open front door.

"First of all, I brought you some wood." He smiled at the pile he'd just stacked neatly to the right of her porch.

"And secondly?"

Unable to help himself, he grinned even bigger. "Secondly, you know I had no choice. I couldn't stay away."

But instead of her looking pleased with

his pronouncement, she looked even more pained.

"Becca, please let me in. It's freezing cold out here."

After a long hesitation, she opened the door and stepped to one side.

"Rebecca?" her mother called out from a back room.

"It's nothing, Mamm. Caleb is here. Again." Narrowing her eyes at him, she added, "He won't be staying long."

Mildly irritated by her words—but even more depressed about the way she was pushing him away—Caleb marched into her living room and sat down.

She followed at a far slower pace. "What do you think you are doing?"

"Making myself at home. Come sit down, Becca," he said before she could dart away. He patted the space on the couch beside him.

She sat across the room from him on an uncomfortable-looking wooden stool. Perched there, she looked like she wanted to leave his company as soon as she could.

Which made him even more depressed.

"Are you afraid of me now?" he asked.

"Of course not."

Worry filled him as he tried to figure out the problem. "Then why are you acting so skittish? Do you not trust me?"

"I trust you."

"Then what is it?" he pressed. "Why are you acting so distant? I can't read your mind, you know."

"Caleb, what do you want me to say? I'm embarrassed." As she paused, her gaze darted beyond him. Like she was hoping for guidance from a higher power.

When she met his gaze again, her expression was sharper, his voice far more bitter. "But you surely know that, right? I never wanted you to know where I lived."

"I don't care, Becca. I promise you, I don't. Besides, there's nothing wrong with this place."

Red stained her cheeks as her expression finally softened.

"I think there is. I think there's everything wrong with this place. I wish we were back at our old house. But it wasn't possible when my *daed* got laid off."

"All that matters is that you're safe and happy. That's all I care about, Rebecca."

"I realize that. But still . . . I didn't want

you to know the truth about my life. Or the truth about what I was doing." She swallowed again, the muscles in her throat working as she tried to catch her breath. Then she added, "Please answer me honestly. Do ya think I'm terrible for giving myself a Christmas basket?"

"No." He meant it, too. He wanted to give her whatever he could to make her happier. He hated the idea of her going without.

Hesitantly, she said, "Caleb, you should know something. I came up with the Christmas basket idea for selfish reasons. I started realizing that there was nothing left over after my parents paid the rent on our place. My *mamm* told me and Mandy that things would be hard this Christmas. Everyone looked so sad."

After darting a look behind her, she left the rickety stool and moved to the space next to him on the couch. "I didn't want my mother to feel bad about our situation. I didn't start out meaning to be selfish and only think about myself. I promise you, I wasn't."

He didn't think Rebecca could be selfish if she tried. "I think what you created was amazing." Unable to help himself, he traced the path of a tear on her cheek. "No matter what the reasons, you helped a lot of families with these baskets, Rebecca. You should feel proud of yourself. I'm proud of you."

But instead of looking reassured and calmed by his praise, she rolled her eyes. "You shouldn't feel proud. I'm sure God is disappointed in me."

"Never."

Lowering her voice, she said, "There was a tiny part of me that was excited about the contents of the baskets. I wanted to eat Mrs. Miller's bread. I wanted to have some fresh food instead of another night of leftovers. A better person would have only been thinking of others."

"Perhaps not."

"Truly?"

Doubt and a small seed of hope lit her eyes, making Caleb's heart melt all over again. The closer they became, the more his feelings for her grew. He loved how she thought of others and was a tiny bit shy. He loved how she was strong enough to do something to help her family, but so self-effacing that she didn't seek recognition. "Rebecca, you have to know . . . if you and your family had let others know of your difficult times, everyone in the community would have given you things without you asking. People like to reach out to others. People like to give."

She shrugged. "Maybe."

"Come now. You were as happy as I was when we gave away the other baskets."

"You're right. I was happy . . . But that's different. It's far easier to give than to receive."

"Sometimes I think it's pride that prevents us all from asking our friends and loved ones for help. Maybe refusing the help and kindness of others is a selfish act, too."

"You sound as if you know something about all this."

"I do. When I was struggling with whether or not I should join the church, I had to let down my pride enough to let other people help me. That takes courage. But only then did I find myself."

"Maybe that's what I'm going through?"

"I think so."

Caleb wasn't sure how good he was at all this, but he knew without a doubt that it was time to let his pride fall and take a chance. It was time to let her know the true extent of his feelings, even if he shocked her and embarrassed them both. Taking a deep breath, he reached for her closest hand and dove in. “Rebecca, I love you.”

Just like that, her eyes widened and her mouth went slack.

Obviously he was no Romeo. Feeling dumb, he began talking quickly. “I’ve been trying to figure out how to tell you that eventually I want to court you and marry you.”

Tears filled her eyes, but he wasn’t sure if they were happy ones or sad.

He swallowed, feeling like he was falling backward into a terribly big hole. “There’s nothing you could do that would make me think badly of you. Or be disappointed in you. Certainly not you doing something so special as making beautiful baskets for people in need.” Then, because she was staring at him in wonder, he said the words again. Thinking that maybe with practice, they would be easy to say out loud. “If anything, Rebecca, I love you more for what you’ve been doing.”

“Are your parents upset?”

"About my feelings for you?" When she nodded, he let himself smile. "Becca, they don't know how I feel. I've certainly never told them."

"You haven't. Really?"

"I promise you, I haven't. What I feel for you is private. Special between you and me. I wasn't going to tell anyone my feelings until I told you. Even though it took me a while." He reached for her other hand and smiled slightly when she folded her fingers around his palms. Once again, he couldn't help noticing how soft her hands were in his. How small and delicate. He rubbed a thumb over one of her knuckles.

"Now I'm the one who's embarrassed. Have I scared you with my . . . enthusiasm?"

"Nee." Blue eyes glowed as a pink sheen glossed her cheeks again. Shyly, she stared down at their joined hands. Sighed.

The silence between them was filled with wonder.

Afraid to say much more, he decided to wait for her to speak. Though she wasn't a chatterbox by any stretch of the imagination, he hoped she would become one, at least for a little bit. He really didn't want to keep trying to guess what she was thinking.

After glancing toward her mother's room, Rebecca leaned closer. "Caleb, I love you, too," she said.

"Yeah?"

The smile that lit her face told him everything that he needed to know.

Instincts rolled through him, and before he could caution himself, before he could tell himself not to do it, he closed the gap between them and carefully pressed his lips to hers. Her lips were soft and slightly parted under his own.

Sweet.

After a few more seconds he pulled away and stared at her wide open eyes.

He now knew without a doubt that no other girl would ever claim his heart. Suddenly, he remembered thinking about all the prayers he'd had over the last year. When he couldn't decide whether God wanted him to be English or Amish. When he didn't know whether he should farm or work in the store—and how empty he'd felt when he'd realized he didn't want to do either occupation.

And in the middle of it all, he'd asked

the Lord for guidance. And choices. And God had done that and more. He'd given him a conversation with his father that had been meaningful and strong. God had provided him with a decent manager at the brickyard who had allowed him to begin apprenticing at the factory right away. Though the work wasn't all that hard—much of the time he only stacked bricks—he was learning much about the job. The other day he even worked by a manager's side at the end of the assembly line, learning how to inspect the bricks and finished pallets.

And God had given his family the wisdom to let him go and make his own mistakes and blunders.

And almost right away, the Lord brought Caleb to Mrs. Miller's house . . . and he'd met Rebecca.

Ever since then, he'd never looked back.

Suddenly, it didn't matter if he was too young, or too short on life experiences. He knew deep inside himself that he didn't need anything else. He knew what he wanted.

But more important, he knew what felt right. So right. With her. Wrapping an arm around her shoulders, he pressed her closer. And went in for another kiss.

Surely nothing was sweeter than kissing Rebecca.

"Caleb, do you need anything?" Mrs. Yoder said as she walked down the hall.

Like a jackrabbit, Rebecca leapt away from him.

Her mother's eyes narrowed as she joined them in the room. "What's going on?"

Face burning, Caleb slowly got to his feet. More than ready to accept the blame for letting things get out of control.

But before he could speak, Rebecca did. "Nothing, Mamm. Caleb came over to ask us to his house for Christmas dinner," she explained, never taking her eyes off of his. "May we go?"

"Caleb, it's all right with your family?"

"Definitely," he fibbed, though he knew in his heart his parents would never turn the Yoders away. "You know how big our family is," he said with a grin. "My parents would enjoy your company. Plus, they asked me to come over here and invite you."

"They did?"

"Of course. I mean, they know how special Rebecca is to me."

Mrs. Yoder stepped forward, her gaze darting from Rebecca to Caleb and back to her daughter again. "And what, may I ask, is going on between the two of you?"

This time Caleb knew he was blushing. "I . . . I like Rebecca very much. I was just telling her that."

"We're in love, Mamm," Rebecca said with a glowing smile.

"Love?" Mrs. Yoder gripped the back of the chair in front of her. Hard. Caleb wasn't sure if that meant she was shocked or angry or amused . . . or maybe all three.

He didn't blame her mother for looking so skeptical. All he could do was attempt to explain himself. "One day, I'm going to marry her."

"One day, hmm?" She looked back and forth at the two of them and smiled. "Those are mighty big plans."

"I love him, Mamm. I can't help it." Rebecca smiled his way. Her smile was so sure and perfect, it made him feel ten feet tall.

"Well, let's just hope the wedding isn't tomorrow."

"It won't be," Caleb assured quickly.

"Well, that is something, ain't so? Now what time should we arrive?"

"Two?"

"We'll be there. Now daughter, if Caleb stays longer, I'm going to want your sister to join you. You've probably gotten close enough on the couch for one day."

It was now official. He was not going to be able to look at Rebecca's mother without his ears turning red ever again. "I'd best be getting on my way. See you tomorrow, Becca?"

She scampered back to his side. "*Jah,* Caleb. I will see you on Christmas Day." Looking over her shoulder, she said to her *mamm*, "I'm just going to tell Caleb goodbye now."

"Quickly, daughter," her mother warned, but then turned and walked away. Leaving them alone for a few last precious seconds.

"I'm glad you came over," she said as she walked him to the door.

"Me, too." For a moment, he considered not touching her. But suddenly, he realized he couldn't not touch her. Gently, he pulled her into a hug and pressed his lips to her cheek. "Have a good night."

"I will."

"I love you." He couldn't help but tell her again. And again.

"I love you, too, Caleb," she murmured.

The last thing he saw before he closed the door behind him was the very sweet smile of hope.

Making him feel like the luckiest man in the world.

Chapter Eighteen

Christmas Eve

She was rushing around like her feet were on fire, Lilly thought as she scampered through a pair of parked cars and darted toward a fancy home-goods store. She needed to get a tablecloth for their Christmas dinner. Everything needed to be as pretty as possible. And as bright and cheery as she could make it so Robert wouldn't be too disappointed that it was just the two of them.

As the hem of her dress got soaked and slapped against her calves, she wished she had on her old jeans and boots. They would be perfect for today. Warmer, too. Shivering, she pulled out her list, determined to only get what was on it and then leave, when she heard a laugh she'd know anywhere.

"Lilly Allen, only you would be stopping in the middle of the sidewalk to check your list."

With some embarrassment, she saw that Josh was right. Everyone was being forced to walk around her, some even going so far as to have to step onto the street. Quickly, she stepped to the side. "Sorry," she mouthed to an elderly lady approaching. Far more loudly, she replied to one of her best friends in Sugarcreek, "Josh Graber, you are speaking to Lilly Miller now, not Allen."

His smile grew broader. "Oh, I know. I just like to tease ya. Where are you going in such a hurry?"

She pointed to the store they were standing in front of. "Here. Want to come in with me for a sec? It's got to be warmer."

"Sure. I've got a second. Maybe even two." He opened the door and motioned her forward.

When they entered the shop, all kinds of

floral scents surrounded them, making her smile and Josh grimace with distaste. In a display in front of them lay an assortment of old-fashioned-looking angels, each one more beautiful than the last. "Oh, aren't those pretty?"

Josh rolled his eyes. "You may be married now, and a Mennonite, but you're still the same, aren't you? Incorrigible."

"And you still don't appreciate girlish stuff." When they shared a smile again, she said, "So, how are you? Good?"

"Very good. My Gretta is expecting again."

"My mom told me the news. Congratulations."

"*Danke.* We moved to our own place not too far from here. It's nice." He paused. "And how are you doing? I heard you're happy with Robert?"

Lilly noticed that his expression was far more serious, and knew it was because he was genuinely concerned about her. "We're good."

"And his family? Are they giving you much trouble?"

"Oh, you heard about their cool attitude, huh?"

"This is Sugarcreek, Lilly. Gossiping is a favorite pastime. So . . . are things better?"

"Truthfully? No. I know Robert's upset, but for the life of me, I don't know how to fix things."

As more women rushed in and the cluttered store became even more crowded, Josh reached out and squeezed her hand. "Will you take a piece of well-intentioned advice?"

"Sure."

"Don't try to manage it. Things will get better in time. That's all everyone needs."

It sounded too simple. "You think?"

He nodded. "Right now, people aren't quite sure what to make of you two. Some people can't forget that you were English."

"And younger."

Josh nodded, looking glad she understood. "And some aren't going to want to forget about Robert once being married to Grace." He paused, waiting for her to meet his gaze. "But I have a feeling that before long, you two will be Robert and Lilly Miller to everyone."

"Even to his relatives?"

"Even so." He smiled warmly. "See, you don't need to be perfect. Just happy."

"How did you get so full of good advice?"

He winked. "Since I became a father. I'm full of wisdom now," he joked. "I'd better get on my way."

"Thanks for stopping me, Josh," she said. "And thanks for the advice. You helped."

With another smile, he left the store, leaving Lilly to realize that maybe she should practice more patience in everything.

And with that, she walked out of the store. Suddenly realizing that a new tablecloth was not going to make their Christmas dinner even more special.

It was already going to be special enough.

"Mamm, I invited Rebecca Yoder, her sister, and her mother over for Christmas dinner," Caleb said as soon as he got in the house.

His mother set down the spoon she was holding, letting it clatter in her mixing bowl. "You did what?"

Belatedly, he noticed that she had been standing next to Judith in deep conversation. Backing up, he said, "Sorry. You want me to talk to you later?"

"Since your sister and I are working on the dinner and you just added three to it, I would say no."

"What's going on, Caleb?" Judith asked.

He didn't want to embarrass Rebecca by telling both his mother and Judith about the baskets. So instead, he decided to share what he could. "I was just over at Rebecca's. Her *daed* couldn't get away from work, so it's just going to be the three of them. And, Mamm, they weren't going to have a dinner. Not much of one, anyway."

"The Yoders have really been struggling, haven't they?"

Caleb nodded. "You don't mind, do you, Mamm?"

"I don't mind." She pretended to scowl at him. "But you are going to peel potatoes tonight."

"I'll peel as many as you want."

Judith looked him over and then slowly smiled. "You seem different. What happened?"

"Nothing."

"Come on. Tell me."

This wasn't going exactly the way he'd planned. But now he realized he was going to have to tell his parents how he felt about Rebecca. Chances were very good her mother would say something about the plans they announced. "Where's Daed?"

"He's in the barn. Why?"

"I'd rather just talk to you and him. No offense, Judith."

"None taken. But . . . you might as well tell us."

"I don't think so . . ."

"Are you sure? Daed and I will talk to you tonight as long as you want. But I promise you, Judith is a *gut* listener. Especially if you have a problem."

"It's not a problem."

Judith raised an eyebrow. "Then?"

"Rebecca and I have fallen in love. I want to marry her. One day."

As they stared at him in shock, Caleb thought privately to himself that this was the very first time the women in the house had been struck silent. He backed up.

"I'm going to talk to Daed."

Weakly, his mother nodded. "*Sur gut,*

Caleb. I think . . . I think that would be a *gut* idea."

As he turned to go back out, Judith stopped him.

"Caleb, you're sure about your feelings, aren't you?"

"I'm more sure of my feelings for her than I've been about most anything. From the moment I saw Rebecca at Mrs. Miller's house last year, I knew I wanted to be in her life." Though he feared he looked like a grinning fool, he added, "Now she feels the same way."

"And you're not scared?"

Looking at his sister, he suddenly realized that she wasn't questioning him, she was questioning herself. Trying to understand her feelings and needing advice. Raising his chin, he said, "I've never been less scared about anything. With Rebecca, I'm happy."

He left then, the cold flecks of snow cooling his cheeks.

Judith could have sworn she felt her chin drop to the floor as her brother left. Her younger brother . . . who suddenly sounded like the wisest man she'd ever met. "Mamm, can you believe that?" she whispered.

Looking bemused, her mother picked up her rolling pin again. "I'm surprised, that is true. But not altogether shocked."

"What do you think Daed is going to say? Do you think he'll tell Caleb that he mustn't see her anymore?"

"Not at all." She put her rolling pin back down. "Judith, why would you imagine that we wouldn't want Caleb to be happy? Especially with a wonderful girl like Rebecca Yoder?" After a moment's pause, she added, "A wonderful-*gut* Amish girl."

"They are so young. And Mamm, Caleb is talking about marriage."

"They are young, but not too young. And marriage is a *gut* thing. Besides, our Caleb did quite a bit of growing last year, don't you think? Perhaps he is ready."

"You think he's serious, don't you?'

"Of course I do. And if I've learned anything over the years, it's that it is not my place to try to tell someone how to feel. Or what they should believe. Or what they should do. Each of us walks our own path with the Lord. I've found it's best to stay out of everyone else's path. All that happens when you try to get in the middle of it is that you get run over."

Judith grinned. "You are a *shmeaht frau*."

"Indeed, I am a smart woman. I'm glad you are finally realizing that." She returned her daughter's smile, then once again picked up her rolling pin and started rolling out pie crust. "Now, dear daughter, what are you going to do about Ben Knox?"

Judith picked up the paring knife and went back to work peeling apples, still hoping to put off the conversation she knew was coming. "Maybe we should make a pecan pie, too?"

"*Jah.* That would be good. Now answer, Judith."

"There's not much for me to say. I already told you that he doesn't want to come over."

"But you didn't tell me his reasons."

"He said Christmas is just another day," she blurted, then said, "But I know he didn't mean that. I think he only said that because he was trying to shield himself."

"From what?"

"From getting hurt. Maybe from having me be hurt, too. Mamm, Ben said Christmas should only be for family, and we weren't his family."

"Ah. And then what did you say?"

Curiously, Judith stared at her mother. “What could I say? It doesn’t matter if I want him here or not. He’s right. He isn’t part of our family, and I can’t force him to do something he doesn’t want to do.”

But instead of agreeing with Judith, her mother looked at her curiously. “How do you feel about Ben, daughter?”

“I told you.”

“Nee.” She shook her head impatiently. “I mean, how do you feel about him, truly? In your heart?”

Giddy. She felt giddy around him. And drawn toward him. And nervous and awkward. And pretty. “Everything,” she mumbled. “When I’m with Ben, I feel confused and sure. Beautiful and clumsy . . .” Her voice drifted off. “How in the world can Caleb feel so sure while I feel so uncertain?”

“Well, he has known Rebecca longer.”

“I went to school with Ben. Plus, I’m older.” Though, even as she explained herself, she knew her reasons weren’t justified. The Ben she knew was different than the boy he’d been.

And, she was coming to find out, she was different than she used to be, too.

"By almost two years, even." It was obvious that her mother was trying not to laugh, which made Judith even more confused. What was she trying so hard not to say?

"What should I do, Mamm? You and Daed asked him here. I asked him, too. He said no."

"I feel bad that he refused our invitation, but that is not the reason to try to convince him to change his mind."

"I feel sorry for Ben."

"Don't ask him here out of pity, Judith. He is a man of pride, yes?"

"Mamm, I don't understand what you want me to say?"

Looking a bit impatient, her mother cast her a knowing look. "Don't you have another reason to want him nearby?"

"I do." Gathering her courage, she said, "Even though it doesn't make sense, I want him to come over because the day won't seem right without him here. I like being around him."

The lines around her mother's mouth eased. Just as if Judith was finally telling her what she'd wanted to hear. "Then tell him that."

"You think so? Truly?"

"Definitely. The worst that could happen is that he still won't want to come over."

No, the worst would be that he refused to see her again. But . . . wasn't that what he was doing anyhow? Wasn't he unwilling to see her now? And pushing away any plans to see her in the future?

But what if things changed? What if Christmas Day wasn't the end of their relationship . . . but merely the beginning?

Excitement infused her as she imagined the possibilities of getting everything she wanted with Ben. "Mamm, do you think I should go over tomorrow and let him know?"

"Not at all."

Disappointment flooded her. For a moment there, she'd been so sure her mother had understood . . .

Beaming brightly, her mother added, "You should go right now. Go to the barn and ask your father or your brother or even Tim to go with you. Or even better, go next door and ask one of the Allens to drive you over."

"You don't think they'd mind?"

"It's only four o'clock. If you promise to

be quick I don't think they'd mind at all. Besides, they'll tell you if they do. Now go and ask. And when you see that man, talk some sense into Benjamin Knox."

"Do you think it will work?'

"Judith, if I know anything, it's that when you make your mind up, you can do anything you'd like. Now go, bring Ben home, and come back to work." Smiling softly, she added, "Plus, tell Ben he's going to have to peel potatoes."

"I thought Caleb—"

"I think Caleb's going to be too busy with his father to help in the kitchen," she said with a twinkle in her eye.

Chapter Nineteen

Ben was mighty proud of himself for not grabbing Judith the moment he saw her and holding her close. Instead, he clutched the frame of the front door and pretended her appearance hadn't taken his breath away. "This is a surprise. Did you need something?"

"I want you to come to our house for Christmas. Pack a bag and come with me."

She sounded so forceful, so sure of herself, he had to smile. "Just like that?"

She looked over her shoulder a little circumspectly, then finally shrugged. "Pretty much."

When she looked over her shoulder again, he craned his neck to try to see what she was looking at. "How did you get here?"

"My English neighbor. Charlie Allen. He lives next door. When I asked him if he could possibly run me over, he agreed."

"That was kind of him."

"It was." She shifted, looking wary. "However, if you could hurry, I'd appreciate it. He's got plans with his girlfriend."

So. Just hours after they'd agreed to not see each other, she had returned. With her English neighbor in tow. And once more, she was ordering him to get his things together. Because her neighbor had a date. "Judith, this . . . this action of yours has made it official: you're crazy."

As he'd hoped, she looked peeved. "I most assuredly am not. I simply want you to change your mind. Quickly."

"And I told you that I wouldn't come over. I gave you reasons. Now you show up, in your English neighbor's car, and pretty much boss me around, telling me I should hurry. Because Charlie has plans."

"It's not just like that. You know it."

"Where did I get things wrong?" He teased.

"What you need to do, Ben Knox, is stop being so stubborn and face facts."

He leaned closer. Not only to press his point but to smell the fresh fragrance of her shampoo. "I need to stop being so stubborn?" Looking into her blue eyes, he thought about her character, about how hard she worked. How much she gave of herself to others.

And how little he trusted others.

"Judith, don't you see? It doesn't matter what you want . . . or what I want. This—this being together ain't right. There's no future in it."

Pain flashed in her eyes before she turned her back on him. His own pain mirrored hers as he realized he was about to get his way.

Within seconds, she was going to leave.

He was going to get his wish—to be stupid and alone on Christmas. He was pushing away the only opportunity he was going to have to get to be with her.

Say something, his conscience urged. Or maybe it was the devil inside of him . . . pushing him to try to obtain something that wasn't right? But would something of the devil make him feel so good as Judith did?

"Judith," he said. "Look. I'm sorry if I seem abrupt, but I'm only trying to do what is best for both of us."

To his amazement, she turned right back around and took two steps closer. "Is that what you're doing?"

He could no more prevent his hands from reaching for her waist than he could prevent Christmas from coming the next day. "I'm t-trying," he sputtered.

Of course, at the moment, he'd forgotten what he was trying to do . . .

With a fierce look of determination, Judith stepped closer. She paused for a brief second, then pressed her hands to his shoulders and kissed him.

Right there on his front stoop. With Charlie the *Englischer* looking on.

Unable to help himself, he kissed her right back. He wasn't all that book smart. He'd made more than his fair share of bad choices. But he wasn't that big of a fool. Her lips were as soft as he'd imagined, her body as pliant and feminine in his arms as he'd dreamt it would be.

One short, chaste kiss led to another. Slowly, the kisses melted into something his dreams had been made of. As his eyes drifted closed, all the pain from his past—and the worries about what could ever hope to be—slowly drifted away. All he could think about was her. *Judith Graber.*

When she lifted her lips, her cheeks were flushed. Beautiful. But her eyes held a hundred doubts and more than a few regrets. "Ben, I'm so sorry. I don't know why—"

"Never apologize for that." Instead of letting her worry more, he pulled her closer. Carefully lowered his head, and kissed her again.

And yes . . . the moment was as sweet as it had been before. Time seemed to stand still. But all too soon he knew that they were getting carried away. When he broke away, he knew it was for the best.

"Wait right here. Or go wait in the car," he said. "It won't take me five minutes to get my bag."

"You're coming over. With me? Now?"

"I had better, don't you think? I mean, if I refuse you, there's no telling who else you're going to attack at their front doors?"

"Attack?" While she sputtered, he ran to his room, suddenly feeling lighthearted and hopeful.

After retrieving his bag, he saw that she

was still standing in his doorway. She looked flushed and bright and embarrassed.

"Ben, perhaps we should talk."

"Let's not. Not yet, anyway." He locked the door behind him, then walked to her side, smiling all the while. "We'll talk more about this later, but please, don't be embarrassed."

"Are you upset with me?"

"Judith Graber, you're the prettiest thing I've ever seen in my life. Years ago, I wished we could be friends. And now here you are, seeking me out, asking me to spend Christmas with you? And kissing me? Holding me like I'm worthwhile? I feel like the luckiest man in the world."

"Truly?"

"What am I going to do with you? Do you think I would have grabbed my bag if I'd been upset? You obviously need to be around me a whole lot more."

Tucking her chin, she smiled. When they got to her friend's car, she introduced him to Charlie.

"Good to meet you," Ben said.

After first giving a fond look to Judith, Charlie grinned. "I'm glad you made up your mind quickly. Ben, Merry Christmas."

"Merry Christmas to you."

As the *Englischer* pulled away from the curb, he chuckled under his breath. "Judith, just to let you know, Lilly owes me a buck."

"And why is that?"

"She thought it would take you at least ten minutes to convince Ben here to come home with you."

"And how long did you guess?" she asked, her voice sharp, but Ben realized it did not sound upset.

Charlie pointed to the clock in the middle of his truck's dashboard. "Under five. Ben, she reeled you in in four minutes flat. It was impressive."

"I can be too pushy sometimes. Are you mad?" she whispered in Ben's ear.

"Me? *Nee.*" The guy's humor was too infectious, Judith's happiness was too transparent, and the sense of finally belonging was so right he couldn't even pretend to be offended.

"I think it's funny. And, if you want to know the truth, I think I made the smartest decision I have in weeks." And to his surprise, he meant every word.

* * *

"Daed, can I tell ya something?" Caleb asked, as he helped his father clean out the stall.

"You don't have to ask. Ever." Pulling out a rake, he began raking out fresh straw. "Son, you know you can always tell me whatever you want."

Automatically, Caleb claimed the rake and took over the job. "This—I mean, what's on my mind—it's a little different, though."

"How so?"

"Well, it's private. Really private. And personal." Thinking about it, he amended his words. "I mean, it's a secret. Of a sort."

Opening the stall door, his father gestured for Caleb to step out. He followed behind. "Son, you are not making a bit of sense. Stop beating around the bush and start talking."

Caleb sighed. His dad was right. "Here it is. If I tell you something, will you promise to hear me out before you get mad?

"Well, now, I'm not rightly sure I can make that promise. It depends on what you have to tell me. Now, what is on your mind?"

"Rebecca Yoder is on my mind. And her mother."

"What about them?"

Looking into his father's eyes, Caleb saw nothing but a gentle curiosity, framed with concern. That gave him the courage to tell the whole truth. "It turns out that Rebecca started that basket program because her family needed a charity basket. She didn't know of another way to help her *mamm*. Mrs. Yoder is a proud woman."

"I have to admire that. Each of us is proud. It's hard to accept things, especially if we don't feel like we deserve them."

"They're going through a really tough time, Daed. Mr. Yoder found work, but it's up by Toledo. He can't even afford to travel home for Christmas."

"And that's why you want them to come over for Christmas?"

"Partly." Now that he'd begun telling the truth, Caleb decided to start sharing the rest of it, too. "The other part of the reason is that I just want to be around Rebecca. I like her a lot. I mean, I think I love her. No, I mean I know I love her. I mean, I do. A lot."

"She sounds like a wonderful girl."

"She is. But Daed, it's like this. Rebecca feels like I wouldn't want her now that I know they needed help. But that don't worry me none. It's not her fault."

"Many people are struggling now."

Caleb was so glad his *daed* understood. "I know! Nothing about that matters to me. But I still get the sense that she wishes things were different."

Instead of brushing off his worry, Caleb watched his father rock back slightly on his feet and think about that for a moment. Then he spoke. "Perhaps you don't need to be worrying so much."

"Why not?"

"It seems to me that God can do that worrying far better than you ever could. He will help Rebecca, Caleb. Don't you doubt that. He's with us always."

"You sure about that?"

Instead of berating him for his lack of faith, his *daed* merely smiled. "I'm as sure about that as I've been about anything. I know He's watching and helping us, Caleb."

With a wink, he pressed his gloved hand on his shoulder. "Especially on Christmas Day."

His father's words were full of wisdom. And, he noticed, not very negative.

"Daed, you're not worried about me being too young, are you?"

"I'd be lying if I said I wasn't worried about your age, but I also have a feeling my concerns are out of my hands. You've grown up a lot, and now have a good job at the brickyard. When the time is right for you and Rebecca, I have a feeling your mother and I will find the time to be just right, too."

Tears pricked Caleb's eyes and he blinked them fast so his father wouldn't see. For his *daed* to have such confidence in him was a blessing. And wonderful.

At the moment, he felt like he'd been given his father's complete trust—and that felt like one of the most wonderful gifts he'd ever received.

Chapter Twenty

Christmas Day

Lilly was still in her pajamas at ten A.M. "I feel so lazy, Robert," she proclaimed even as she stretched her legs farther under the quilt on the couch.

"You shouldn't," he replied over his second cup of coffee. As he stretched out beside her, he continued. "I'm glad you are taking care of yourself. It is snowing outside and we are cozy in here together. There's no reason for you to worry about getting dressed."

"Maybe. Or maybe not . . ." All morning,

everything had been perfect. Robert had gotten up and made coffee, then brought her a cup to sip while she was still nestled inside a snug bed of flannel sheets.

Later, she'd made them breakfast and they'd sat in front of the back window of his house and watched the snow fall. When a pair of deer wandered near, nosing the blanketed bushes and shrubs circling the yard, there didn't seem to be a better activity than watching them.

Now they were sitting in the living room. "Are you ready to open presents?" she asked.

"I am. I wondered when you were going to be ready to open gifts."

"I've been so excited, I didn't want to rush things. But now I don't think I can wait any longer."

"Then, let's do it. You first."

"Okay. Scampering to the hall closet, she pulled down the pretty gold-wrapped box. "Here you go, Robert."

He looked up at her and smiled. "I have to admit to being very curious about this gift. All month you've looked like you lost your best friend."

"I wanted to get you something special

and nothing seemed good enough. Until this."

"You do realize I meant what I said, yes? I really do feel like I have the best Christmas gift of all. You."

That was Robert. So serious. So sincere. "I know what you said. And I'm grateful for you. And I feel the same way, too. Of course. But there's only one first Christmas you know." She placed the box in his lap, then scampered on the couch next to him. "Open it."

Obediently, he began pulling off the gold bow, then wrapping paper. He paused when he noticed the name on the outside of the box. "Lilly?"

She'd never been so proud. "Open it."

Slowly, he opened the lid. Then he stared in surprise. "It's a watch."

"Yes. As soon as you said yours got crushed, I knew I wanted to give you something special, something you could give your son . . . if God one day blesses us with one. Do you like it?"

He carefully removed it from the case and held it up by its bracelet. "It's very fine."

Very fine? "It's stainless steel. And waterproof. And the jeweler said it has a lifetime warranty. If it breaks, they'll repair it for free."

His white teeth flashed as he smiled her way, then awkwardly unclasped it. Slid it on his left wrist.

Unable to stop herself, she grabbed hold of his wrist and helped him clasp it. "Hey, it looks like it fits just fine. I was worried it might be too small."

"Too small?"

"You've got big wrists."

Staring at his wrist, he said, "This watch, it's going to take some getting used to."

Her heart sank. "Do you not like it? Is it too much of a difference from your pocket watch? I guess I was only thinking about what you can do now, not what you wanted."

"Because I'm Mennonite now?"

Did he sound bitter? "Yes," she mumbled. "You've been enjoying jeans so much, I started thinking a watch would be a good thing. But don't worry. We can return it."

"I'm not going to return it." Moving close, he pressed his lips to her brow. "I love it. It is truly special."

She heaved a sigh of relief. "Oh, thank goodness. I'm so glad you like it! I've been so worried."

"It looks terribly expensive."

She didn't know how to respond to that. It had been expensive. Was Robert worried she'd taken money from their savings account? "Don't worry, I was able to pay for it from some of my own money."

"From some of your own?"

If anything, he looked even more worried.

"Robert, please, do you like it?"

After taking another long look at his wrist, he linked his fingers around one of hers and pulled her close to him. "Very much so. It is a wonderful-*gut* Christmas gift, Lilly."

She sighed in relief. "I'm so glad."

"So are you ready for your turn now?"

"Yes."

"I think we should draw this out a bit."

"Why? I've been wondering all month what you've been making for me." She knew she was as antsy as a child but she really was excited. "Go get it."

He laughed. "Why don't you put some of your Christmas music on? I've started to like some of the pretty songs, like 'Silent Night.'"

It was as if a heavy shutter had just landed on her insides. Just like that, she felt her excitement deflate. "There's no need."

"I know, but I know you like to listen to the music so much."

"Robert, I told you that I wasn't going to use my computer so much," she hedged. Now was definitely not the time to tell him that she had sold the computer to pay for the watch.

"And I told you that your using your computer didn't bother me."

"I'm not going to get it out."

"Perhaps you'll change your mind," he said cryptically as he walked to the back bedroom.

"Especially now that you have this," he said with a flourish of his hand.

She jumped to her feet. "What? Walking toward the room, she peeked inside and stopped abruptly. "Robert, you made me a desk?"

All smiles, he wrapped an arm around her waist and pulled her in closer. "I did. It's for your computer."

"What?"

"Look." He opened up the door center drawer, slid it out then pulled the face of it down flat. "See? It's for a keyboard. Mr. Allen told me a lot of desks have that now, even for laptops. So you can attach the keyboard."

The lump in her throat seemed to grow double in size. "I . . . it's beautiful."

"It's cherrywood. I thought about maple, then oak, but decided this was the right wood for you." With a loving hand, he caressed the fine wood across the top. "I'm glad you like it."

"I love it. Very much." Unable to stop her tears, she blubbered, "No one's ever given me such a perfect gift."

"Most people don't cry when they receive gifts, Lilly."

She sat on the bed, feeling at a complete loss for words. She wanted to hug Robert and confess all. To tell him that she didn't have her computer anymore.

But the urge to keep her secret close to her chest was just as strong. She so didn't want to disappoint him anymore.

He sat beside her. "What is wrong? You can tell me anything, you know."

He was right. Taking a breath, she made her choice. "I . . . I did something that I know you're going to be upset about." She paused again. Still afraid. "And, well . . . I'm afraid to tell you."

"You couldn't do anything to upset me." Lifting her chin with one finger he looked into her eyes. "Lilly, please stop worrying so much about how I feel about you. You know I love you."

"I know. But still, I don't want you to be upset." Mentally, she chastised herself. She really was making things worse instead of better.

"I won't be upset, Lilly. I promise, no one has made me this happy in so very long."

His words were so sweet. So kind. So everything.

So much more than she deserved. "I can't believe I managed to ruin today."

"Lilly, what? What is wrong?" Impatience laced his words now.

"I sold my computer to buy your watch!" she blurted out.

When he stared at her in shock, she cried even harder. This was horrible. This was the worst Christmas Day in the world.

No matter how hard she tried, it was becoming painfully obvious that she was the absolute worst wife for Robert. They were such a mismatch. And any moment now, he was going to be completely certain about that, too.

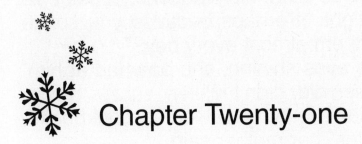

Chapter Twenty-one

Ben knew that Judith Graber was one of the sweetest women he'd ever met. But the way she was looking at him made his stomach twist up in knots and his palms sweat.

And what was worse, her whole family was watching him do it.

"Ben, this is the best present in the world." Holding the two cookbooks in her lap like they were made of glass, she gazed at him in wonder. "How did you know these books were just what I wanted?"

Now he was embarrassed. After all . . . they were just cookbooks. Not anything special. To cover his emotions, he kept his voice light. “Perhaps because you spoke about them almost every day?”

Blue eyes shining, she beamed at him. “I guess I did, didn’t I?”

“I didn’t know you wanted cookbooks, daughter,” her mother said.

“That’s because I didn’t tell you. I thought you might think they were silly.”

Taking one of the books from her, she flipped it open then looked at Judith in confusion. “Why would I think that?”

“Because you’ve taught me how to cook. And, well, I’ve never seen you use a cookbook, ever.”

“I read them on occasion. I think they’re fine books, Judith. I’m sure *I’m* going to want to read them.”

“Me, too,” Clara said with a kind smile in Ben’s direction. “I don’t know of a woman who doesn’t appreciate some new recipes.”

“You did a good job with your present,” Gretta murmured next to him. A kind smile was in her voice. Just like she knew what it was like to be a newcomer to the gregarious group.

“They were just books.” Eager to get the attention away from him, he leaned toward

Maggie. "Are you ever going to open your gift from me?"

"Uh-huh. But I wanted your help."

"What?" He looked to others for help. "You can't rip off wrapping paper yourself?"

"She likes to sit with the person who gave her the gift," Gretta explained. "It means a lot to her."

Maggie stood in front of him, bottom lip tucked in her mouth. Looking at him in expectation.

Opening his arms, he smiled. "Come here, Miss Maggie. I'd love for you to sit with me."

As the little girl looked at him with such trust and affection, Ben felt his heart melt. While Judith had captured his heart and tied it in knots, this little girl seemed to have given her heart to him decorated in a sweet pink ribbon. A perfect gift.

She scrambled on his lap and smiled sweetly at him. "Ben, open it."

"All right."

Together, his big fingers intertwined with her delicate ones. Untying the red ribbon clumsily. Then opening up the cardboard box he'd put his gift in.

"It's a donkey!"

"It is. I didn't see one of those when we were playing animals the other day."

One perfect eyebrow lifted, disappearing under her *kapp*. "Do you like donkeys?"

"*Verra* much so. After all, that's what Mary rode into Bethlehem, right?'

Somberly, Maggie nodded.

After they talked a bit more, the last of the gift giving was over. Ben let himself relax as he realized he'd made it through the family event without making a fool of himself.

Yet.

Ben tensed when Mr. Graber picked up his large, well-worn Bible and cleared his throat. Uh-oh. Was this yet another family tradition he was going to have to fumble through?

"I'm thinking since Ben here is talking about donkeys and Mary and all," he paused, glancing Ben's way with half a smile, "it's probably time to read our Christmas story."

Ben felt himself relax as he finally realized the intent. When little Maggie scooted closer to him, backing up until her back touched his knee, he found himself resting his hand on her shoulder. But whether it was to comfort her or assure him, he wasn't sure.

"I thought this year we'd read from the Book of Matthew," Mr. Graber said. "For some reason, I've been thinking about that bright star in the East and how the wise men had such a great faith that they followed it without hesitation."

"The star was really bright and pretty, Daed," Maggie said, her voice as sweetly pure and bright as any star in the sky.

Everyone in the room smiled.

"I think you must be right, Maggie," Mr. Graber said, then slipped his glasses more securely over his nose and found the passage he was looking for with his finger. "Here we go.

" 'When the wise men saw the star, they were filled with joy. They came to the house where the child was and saw him with his mother, Mary, and they bowed down and worshiped him. They opened their gifts and gave him treasures of gold, frankincense, and myrrh . . ."

As Maggie's back straightened and Anson blurted that he still didn't understand what "myrrh" was, the whole room burst into discussion. Ben closed his eyes and felt a peace he'd never imagined existed.

Conversations floated around him, more about stars and Jesus and wise men . . . and Ben thought about Judith. And how in many ways, she'd been a bright star in his life.

If nothing else, she'd guided him toward a feeling of hope. That there was more to life than painful memories and feelings of doubt and insecurity.

Then, just as if he'd willed her to, someone sat down beside him. "I'm so glad you're here. I would have hated to do all this without you." Judith looked so pretty sitting next to him; she had on a new dress—or at least one he'd never seen before. It was a deep navy blue. And that blue did amazing things to her eyes, making them shine a little deeper . . . and transform his thoughts.

Turning toward her, he attempted to make a little bit of space between them, because she was so close that he couldn't seem to do anything but stare at her. And that was the last thing he wanted to do. Neither she nor her family needed to know just how deep his feelings for her went.

Therefore, he concentrated on keeping his voice light. “I’m glad I’m here, too. Thanks for not giving up on me.” Not liking how that sounded, he rephrased. “I mean, thanks for coming to get me. Even when I told you no.”

“Having you here feels right.” This time she looked just as flustered. “I mean, I’m glad for your friendship.”

“I know what you mean.” It was obvious she was feeling just as confused and torn as he was.

She reached out her hand. He stilled his body, getting ready for her touch. Then, just as suddenly, she dropped her hand. “I should go. I mean, I’ve got to go help in the kitchen.”

“Yes. And I . . . I thought I’d go chop logs.”

She nodded, but then turned to him, nibbling her bottom lip. “But later, maybe the two of us could sit and talk?”

As he looked into her eyes, he knew he’d promise her anything. However, he also knew he needed to keep things easy between them. Simple. “I’d like that,” he said easily.

Just like he received invitations like that all the time.

Chapter Twenty-two

When Lilly finally stopped crying, she lifted her head and stared warily at her husband. “I’m sorry. I really am.”

Robert hung his head. “Don’t be.”

Panic rose in her. “Robert, I’ll do anything to make this better,” she said in a rush. “I promise—”

But when Robert lifted his head, she realized that he was smiling, not glowering. In fact, it actually looked like he was trying not to chuckle.

“Are you amused?”

“Of course.” He stood up and reached for her hand. Then tugged her out of the room, down the hall, and into the living room.

She walked a few paces behind him, letting herself be led. Wondering why he was amused. Wondering where he was leading her to. Finally they stopped in front of the windows.

"Pretty out, ain't so?"

Snow covered every branch. Deer tracks covered the ground in pretty abstract patterns. And, like a beacon of the season, a bright red cardinal sat in a distant pine. "It's a beautiful day."

He cleared his throat. "Last night, I couldn't sleep. After a while, I snuck out of bed and stood right here." He darted a look her way. "The snow had stopped and there were breaks in the clouds."

"What did you see?"

"Stars." He smiled. "And of course, given that it was Christmas Eve, I started thinking about those wise men, following a distant star. Bearing the best gifts they had . . . but not all that sure how they would be received."

"Your gift was perfect, Robert. It was a perfect gift."

"I love my watch, too." Wrapping an arm

around her shoulders, he murmured, "But that isn't what I was thinking. I was thinking that I have a wonderful light here in my life now, too. See, I've always had the bright feeling of the Lord's love. But now I see you and feel the same happy way. You, Lilly, are my bright light. Bringing me happiness."

The words he was saying . . . they were so heartfelt, she almost believed him. "You don't wish I was different? You don't blame me for your family being so distant?"

"I don't want you different. And as for my family? . . ." He shrugged. "I've reached out to them as much as I can. One day, they're going to need to reach out to me, too. I can't make things better all by myself. They need to want to be closer, too."

As she processed his words, he turned away from the windows and braced his two hands on her shoulders. "Lilly Miller, are you ready to finally listen to me? To listen good?"

"I'm listening."

"If you were different, I wouldn't have fallen in love with you. I love your Christmas music and the fact that you try so hard to make me terrible meals. I love that you waitress so well and don't care that I drive so badly. I love your golden curly hair and your chocolate-colored eyes." His hands squeezed harder. Almost hurting. "But, Lilly, do you know what I love most?"

She shook her head. She couldn't imagine.

"I love that you'd be willing to let go of something that means so much to give me a special gift. I will always remember this day."

"I do love the desk. It's beautiful, and it means the world to me that you built it for me . . ."

"You had better, because we are going out tomorrow and buying you a new computer for it." His tender smile matched the way his hands were now sliding down her arms. "And don't even think of telling me no, wife. I have hopes that you might even find new recipes on your Internet."

She laughed and looped her hands around his neck. "There might be hope for me yet!"

Just before he kissed her, he nodded. "I promise, Lilly, if I have you, there's hope for us all. Now kiss me and tell me Merry Christmas."

"Merry Christmas, husband," she murmured, then closed her eyes and kissed him.

And thought that, maybe, this was the most wonderful day in the year after all.

She'd come. Rebecca and her mother and sister. They were standing in the entryway, looking a bit like lost sheep.

Caleb didn't fault their expressions. A noisy family gathering could frighten even the most hardy of spirits.

"Hey, Rebecca," he said. "Hi, Mrs. Yoder. Amanda. Merry Christmas."

"And Merry Christmas to you," Mrs. Yoder said. Looking a bit embarrassed, she added, "Your brother greeted us, but I'm afraid he left before telling us where to put our coats?"

"Joshua?" He couldn't imagine his brother being so rude.

"Anson," Rebecca said with a wink.

His cheeks flushed. "I'm sorry," he said as he held out his hands for their cloaks. "Anson has the manners of a barnyard animal."

"Only sometimes," his mother said with a laugh as she joined them. After greeting the ladies, she said, "Actually, Anson ran to the kitchen to get me. So he might have just a few more manners than the chickens. Now, Caleb, perhaps you'd like to show Rebecca and Amanda around? I'll take Mrs. Yoder into the kitchen."

"Sure." Quickly, he hung up their cloaks on some pegs by the front door, then walked the girls into the family room.

Immediately, Maggie brightened and claimed Amanda's hand. "Come see my donkey!" she said excitedly as she pulled Amanda away.

Which left Rebecca standing alone with Caleb. At last.

"I'm so glad you came," he said.

"Me, too."

He ached to touch her. To brush the stray hair that had fallen across her cheek. To hold her hand. To hold her close.

But even more than that was the urge to look into her eyes and make sure everything between them was still all right. "Becca, about yesterday . . ."

She leaned close. "Do you still love me?" Her voice was merry, but her expression was seeking. Waiting.

"Jah." Honestly, his tongue felt so

thick, that was the best reply he could manage.

"Gut." She leaned a bit closer, bumping his arm lightly with her shoulder. "Then that's all I need to know."

As others approached, and the noise in the living room got a little louder as Clara laughed with Anson, Judith poked her head in. "Rebecca, want to help? We're about to start filling up the serving platters."

"I'd be happy to help," she said. Just like she already belonged. "I'll be right there." When Judith turned away and they were alone again, Rebecca gazed at him. "I'll see you later."

After treating him to yet another beautiful smile, she turned and left. When he was completely alone, Caleb breathed a sigh of relief. Then closed his eyes and praised God.

He was so lucky. So blessed. "Thank you, Lord," he whispered. He wasn't good at fancy prayers, only expressing what was in his heart. He hoped his simple, heartfelt thank-you would be enough.

But then he remembered Rebecca's words and knew it was. He had Rebecca and she had him. They had each other and, once more, were in love. And put like that, well, nothing else mattered.

Supper had been wonderful. Noisy and filled with laughter. The cleaning up hadn't been a hardship, either. Not with everyone there to help.

So, Judith wondered as she stood outside on the front porch, why wasn't she feeling happier?

"Hey. Sister? Are you okay?"

Judith turned to find Caleb standing at the entrance to their home. Behind him, the noise of the crowded house filtered into the air. The dim lights of a dozen candles illuminated his form, making him seem as old and grown up as he now was.

In spite of all their efforts to keep him a child, it was now terribly obvious that Caleb Graber *had* grown up.

"I think so," she said. "I'll be inside in just a minute; I just needed a break. Everything started to feel a little overwhelming."

"What did?" he asked as he walked out to join her. "The noise? The hundred people staring at you, wondering what you were thinking?"

She rolled her eyes. "There's hardly a hundred people in our house." As a burst of laughter floated through the door, she added, "It only seems that way."

He chuckled. "For the first time ever, I'm gettin' a sense of what Tim must have thought when he lived with us the spring he fell in love with Clara. No wonder he spent as much time with her! Our family is large and loud and demanding."

"And we always have been."

He paused. "Have you ever felt like everyone's too nosy, as well?"

"Only when I have secrets," she said with a wink. "Want to join me for a second?"

"Sure." As he walked, he crossed his arms in front of him, obviously trying to get warm.

"You should have put on a coat."

"And you shouldn't have been out here in the first place." When he rested his elbows on the railing beside her, she studied him from the corner of her eye. At first glance, Caleb seemed steady and relaxed. But there also seemed to be a bit of tension emanating from him. "Do you have secrets?"

He shrugged. "Some. About as many as any of us have, I suppose."

"Are yours tonight centered on Rebecca?"

"A little bit." He cracked a knuckle. Then a second. "If you want to know the truth, I haven't been thinking about secrets tonight. Instead, I can't seem to stop thinking about today and the true miracle of it all."

She wasn't quite following him. Today? "The miracle of Christ's birth?"

"*Jah*. But more, too. I feel like today, on His birthday, I finally am at peace. I feel like he's given me the best gift imaginable, you know?"

"His love?"

"*Jah.* And the capacity to love." With the faint glow of the house's candles illuminating his face, he looked at her, true wonder apparent. "Aren't you amazed by it all? That there's room in our hearts for one more person?"

"I'm not sure if I'm feeling the same things you are," she hedged, wondering why she was fighting her feelings, anyway. "Ben and I . . . nothing can become of our relationship."

"Who says?"

"Ben. He's moving, Caleb. His house is up for sale. Soon he'll leave, and he's already told me that when he leaves Sugarcreek, he's not coming back."

"Maybe he'll change his mind. People do."

"Maybe. At first, I thought he had too many bad feelings about Sugarcreek to want to stay. But this past week, he's seemed happy . . ."

"People can change. I did."

Caleb was right. For years he'd been angry and restless, constantly telling them that Sugarcreek wasn't where he belonged. But then a visit with Lilly Allen's English friends changed that. "I had hoped Ben would change his mind. But now I don't know." Too embarrassed to look at him any longer, she stared out straight ahead. "Maybe he's waiting for me to say something. Waiting for me to beg him not to leave."

"It will work out. It has to, you know."

"I hope so. If I keep praying, I think it will."

"If you keep praying, you'll find comfort."

"You sound sure of that."

"I sound sure because I know I'm right. Judith, each of us has prayers just waiting to be answered. And our Lord is only waiting for us to depend on him."

Her little brother was amazing. "Caleb Graber, when did you get so smart?"

"Right about the time everyone stopped telling me I was too young to know my own mind."

"What are you two doing out here?"

Judith turned around to see Joshua hovering in the same doorway Caleb had been in just moments before. "Nothing," she told him. "We're just talking. Thinking out loud."

"And escaping," Caleb blurted. "I'll say it. We're taking a break from the mob inside our home."

"In that case . . . can I join you both?"

"Of course." As her older brother stepped forward and mimicked their stance, leaning on the rails just like she and Caleb were, she couldn't help but wonder what had brought him out to them. "Is everything all right inside?"

"Everything's fine—everyone has settled down and is relaxing. Anson's playing a game with Toby. Gretta and Clara are looking at quilting magazines. Tim is reading a book in the empty kitchen. Ben is looking at Maggie's coloring books." His voice drifted off. "Anyway, I was about to sit down, too. But then I started looking for you two . . . and thinking about how much things have changed for me over the last few years."

"That's only natural," Judith replied. "You've got a baby and another on the way."

"I mean things have changed inside me." He cleared his throat. "There had been a time when I wasn't sure what the right path for me was supposed to be."

"But then you decided," Caleb said.

"I did." After a pause, Joshua added, "I'd like to say that I had a flash of light and that the Lord starting talking in my ear, but it wasn't like that. Instead, it felt more like He was showing me the way in a slow and steady glow. I followed."

"'Glow.' I like that," Judith murmured, thinking that was exactly how she'd felt when she was around Ben. When he was near, she felt more vibrant, more clear, more everything.

As another roar of laughter floated through the house, followed by a crying that could only be from Will, the three of them stepped away from the railing.

"Guess we better go on in," Judith said. "Mamm won't like us out here if there's things that need to be done inside."

"I'm surprised Anson hasn't come looking for us," Caleb murmured.

"He will," Joshua said as he held the door open for them to walk through. "If I've learned anything over the last year, it's that some things never change."

Judith smiled at her brother. "For the first time in a while, I'm glad of that."

"Me, too, sister," Josh said. "Me, too."

Her voice was as clear and bright as the day had been. "Ben?"

He turned to Judith. "Hi," he said from his spot on the floor in front of the Graber's massive brick fireplace. "I thought I'd stay down here for a little longer. I, uh, wasn't quite ready to go to sleep."

"I wasn't, either." To his delight, she sat right down beside him, curling her thick robe around her feet. As the sparkling flames of the fire warmed her, she yawned. "It's late, though."

He glanced at the oak clock on the far wall. "It is. Almost two. We're going to be dead on our feet tomorrow morning."

"I bet you're wishing you'd gone on home, huh?"

"Not at all. It was a wonderful-*gut* day. One of the best Christmases I've ever had." Actually, it was more than that. He'd felt part of the group, part of a family. If he could have made it last another three hours, he would've done so.

"Ben, perhaps you should stay here longer."

He wanted to. But for what? To be an overeager hanger-on to the Grabers? "I promised myself I'd come for Christmas. And Christmas is over. It's time I moved on, too."

She frowned. "But, Ben—"

"Judith, my life ain't like yours. I don't have roots. And, well, the roots I have aren't all that good here. It's time to start over."

"Couldn't you start over here in Sugarcreek?"

Her expression was so earnest, he

wanted to say he could. But where would that get him? Before long, she'd realize he wasn't good enough for her.

And then he would have an even harder time leaving than he was having now.

"Judith, I can't start over here. I'll work tomorrow because I promised your *daed,* but then I'm going to sign the realtor's papers and leave. It's for the best."

Slowly, she got to her feet. "I understand," she murmured, though it was clear from the tone of her voice that she didn't at all.

That was fine, he didn't understand what he was doing, either. Was he running to a new future?

Or merely running from the idea of more pain?

Clambering to his feet, he looked at her one last time in the glow of the fire. And right then and there, he knew he'd never forget this moment. She was so pretty—and represented so much to him.

"Merry Christmas, Judith," he said quietly. The words weren't much, but they were all he had.

She blinked. "And Merry Christmas to you, Ben. *Gut naught.*"

He turned back to the flames so he wouldn't watch her walk away. So he wouldn't be tempted to call her back.

And stood in front of the flames until they died out.

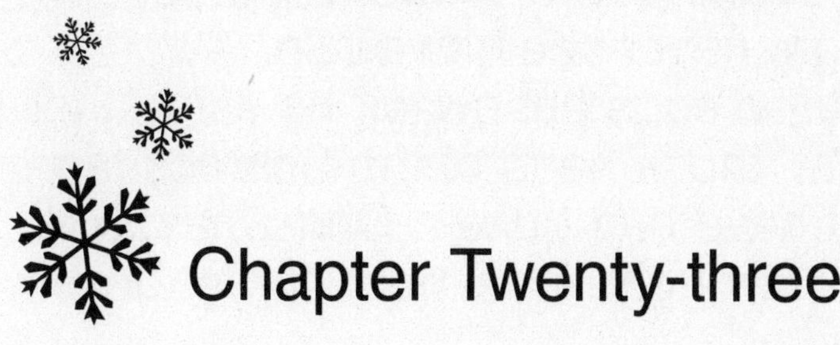

Chapter Twenty-three

The Day After Christmas

It was almost six o'clock. Since they'd arrived at the store that morning, Judith had tried her best to stay all business. Ben had, too.

Keeping things distant and professional hadn't been all that hard, not really. The store had been swamped with customers, all either stopping in for staples or for sales.

But now that Joshua and her father had left, leaving Ben and her to clean up and close, a panic rose inside her.

This evening she would drop him off. And might never see him again.

"I got the eggs put away," he said. "I tell you what, those hens of the Schrock family must have had quite a Christmas. Mrs. Schrock brought in almost three dozen eggs today."

"Ben, don't leave," she blurted.

He stilled. "What?"

"Don't leave—" *me,* she added silently.

"Oh, I'm not leaving yet." He paused at the entrance to the work area in the back of the store. "I know we've still got a lot to do."

Walking toward him, she shook her head. Then finally managed to tell him what she should have told him days before.

Or at the very least, last night.

"I'm not talking about the store. I mean don't leave Sugarcreek." When he blinked, she forced herself to continue. To tell him what was really in her heart—even if it meant she was laying it open to him. "Ben, I mean . . . don't leave *me.*"

He felt his mouth go slack, which was just fine for him. He felt like his mind had gone missing, too.

"Why?" he sputtered.

Judith pursed her lips, then, as if she'd finally come to a great decision, spoke. "Because I can't bear the thought of letting you go."

"I mean, why are you saying all this to me? I thought we'd decided it would be best if I moved on. I thought you understood that it would be best if we didn't hope for anything more."

She shook her head. "*Nee.* You decided that. Not me. I want you here. I think you could have a wonderful-*gut* future here in Sugarcreek." She swallowed. "With me."

With her. He ached to pull her close and tell her that everything she said was right. Perfect . . .

"Ben, you aren't perfect, but neither am I. And I don't know what the future holds for us, only God does. But I do think you returned for a reason."

"Which is?"

"Me. Us. You can't deny it much longer, can you? We have something special."

Judith was right. But was he willing to disappoint her? Because even though he didn't know what the future offered, he was certain he would do that. "Judith, I don't know if I can ever be the man you need me to be."

"Of course you can." Reaching out, she grasped his right arm. Her cool, slim fingers looked so feminine against his blue shirt. It took everything he had not to press his left hand over hers. To keep it there.

"Judith, you see me and you see a man who is grateful. And I am. I'm grateful to your father for the work. And I'm grateful to your family for giving me a Christmas I'll never forget. But that's not enough for you."

"Of course it is. Besides, you're more—"

"You need a better man," he interrupted.

But instead of scaring her away, she turned angry. Pulling her hand away from his arm, she glared. "What kind of man is better than you?"

"A man who already has proven himself to be worthy of you."

"You have. You've proven it with the way you've worked hard here . . . and helped so much around our house. You've proven how worthy you are when you've looked after me and always put my safety first. You've been gentle with Maggie and kind to my mother and wonderful to me."

To his ears, those things sounded insignificant.

"Ben, at first I was thinking I wasn't right for you, either. But that was just my fears talking, not my heart." She took a deep breath and continued. "See, all I've ever wanted was to go home each night to someone who will be there for me, through thick and thin. Who would love me."

He did love her. He knew it as strongly as he knew he would be happy with her for a lifetime. But was that enough? Slowly, he said, "All I've ever wanted was someplace to belong. To be around people who want me. The rest, it doesn't matter all that much to me."

"Then, please stay."

It was the "please" that got to him. So earnestly said, he felt as if his decision was everything to her. Like he mattered.

Filling the silence, she spoke quickly. "Ben, don't sell your house. Don't sell your land. Let me help you with it."

"That house isn't a home, Judith." He didn't even try to hide the disappointment he felt. But he wasn't willing to let her into his life . . . just to watch her hope slide into disappointment as she realized he was never going to be the man she'd hoped he would be.

"But that house can become a home. Ben, all you have to do is stop running and take a chance."

Everything she was saying— Could it be that easy? Was that all possible? It just took the will of a strong woman to know what was important? "I don't know . . . I love you, Judith. But that's not enough."

"I think it is." Her eyes flashed, and he knew right then and there he should have said something more sweet. Far smoother. "Say it again."

"I love you." When she smiled, his heart lifted. But once again, old feelings of insecurities blindsided him. "Judith, see? Here I meant to tell you my feelings in a sweet, tender way. Obviously, I'm messing this up, too."

"Never." Raising her arms out wide, she looked at the building. "You could never disappoint me. See, I don't want the fancy Ben Knox, or the one with all the trimmings. I want the Ben that's like our Christmas. Like an Amish Christmas. Not an English one, with too much fancy dressing and noise and glitter and shininess. I want the Ben I see in front of me now. The man who is a little stark. Without fancy airs or plans. I want you."

"Plain, huh?" He was charmed by her words in spite of himself. "And what kind of Ben is that?"

"The Ben who speaks the truth, even when it hurts. The Ben who wants what is right, even if it isn't the popular thing. The Ben who we all gather around and cherish because he's real. Not fake."

The man she wanted was in some ways the man it was hardest to be. It was still scary to let others see his weaknesses and insecurities. It took courage to let others see his real personality: The man who liked to read books and enjoyed nothing more than being around caring people. The man who wanted to stay in Sugarcreek because Judith Graber was there.

"Are you sure? Because if I stay now I don't think I will have the strength to go."

Yeah, right. Who was he kidding? In his heart, he knew he'd do just about anything to stay with Judith. Even if it meant befriending every person in the town.

Or staying late with her at work. He was willing to do just about anything to make her happy.

"I'm more than sure. I'm positive. See, Ben, I need you here. Before you came back, Sugarcreek was just the town I lived in. Before you came back, my family was just my family—I'd never tried to see them through another's eyes. And Christmas . . . Christmas was simply a day to give thanks and to remember Jesus's birth."

"And now? . . ." He was almost afraid to ask.

"Now Christmas will be all those things, plus the time I first felt like I belonged. And my family will be all the people I love because of their faults. Not in spite of them."

Smiling brightly, she continued. "And this town—Sugarcreek—it will be special to me because of the memories and the people that live here. But most especially, because it's the place to call home. Because it will be your home, too."

Ben curved his arms around Judith and pressed his lips to her brow. Then, carefully, he crossed the store and after doing yet another search, he turned the Open sign to Closed.

Just as the silly bird clock above them chirped six o'clock.

"It's closing time," he announced.

But the smile he sent her way told her so much more. Their day was over, but their life together had just begun.

There, in a small country store in a rather small town called Sugarcreek. Just one day after Christmas, Benjamin Knox had finally discovered the true meaning of the season.

To celebrate Jesus's birth? Yes.

To celebrate life, too? Definitely.

It was the time to give thanks for all of God's wonderful blessings that were bestowed on them all, all the year round.

Turning around, he looked at Judith Graber. She was standing straight and tall and staring at him with such love in her eyes, it fairly took his breath away.

"Are you ready to go home now?" she asked.

"I am," he replied with a smile. Thinking for the first time in his life that the word *home* now meant the world to him.

Dear Reader,

Merry Christmas!

I hope you enjoyed *Christmas in Sugarcreek*. I, for one, loved returning to the setting of the Seasons of Sugarcreek books and catching up with all the characters. Ever since I finished writing *Autumn's Promise*, I knew I needed to tell Judith's story. I felt a little guilty that I'd given so many other people love and romance but had neglected poor Judith! I always thought Judith needed a man who loved her enough to make her smile. I think Ben Knox was perfect for her.

Has your Christmas season been busy? Now that both my children are in college, I've been anticipating the holidays more than usual. I've been planning activities and dinners and gifts and vacations—sometimes even forgetting what my kids want most for Christmas: to be home. They like eating meals that they've had a hundred times. They like being around our dogs, watching TV on the couch, and beating their parents at Scrabble. I love hearing their voices across the room . . . and I especially love just being Mom for a while.

The theme for this novel came from a Christmas sermon at our church. Our pastor talked about the three wise men searching for the star, and gently reminded all of us that there is quite a bit of light and hope inside each of us, too—if we're brave enough to seek it.

So, this Christmas, I hope each of you finds the light that has been guiding you—or, even better, realizes that you are the light that guides others. In addition, I wish you the company of friends and family and too much good food to eat! I wish you happy memories and mistletoe and the time to enjoy it all, too. But most of all, I wish you happiness. That, I think, is a gift that gives back all year round.

With Christmas blessings to you,

Shelley Shepard Gray

PS. I love to hear from readers and send out bookmarks, too! Please visit me at www.shelleyshepardgray.com, on Facebook, or write me at:

Shelley Shepard Gray
10663 Loveland-Madeira Rd. #17,
Loveland, OH 45140

Questions for Discussion

1. The theme of belonging is an almost-constant one in my novels. *Christmas in Sugarcreek* was no exception. Ben, Rebecca, and Lilly all felt that they weren't quite good enough for the people who loved them. Did they change . . . or did their perceptions about themselves change?

2. Writing about Lilly and Robert celebrating their first Christmas together made me nostalgic. Over twenty years ago, my husband and I started several

traditions that have become an integral part of our holiday season. Do you have any traditions that you began? Are there any traditions you wish you could change?

3. The Amish are known to be very giving and charitable people, which is one of the reasons I wanted Caleb and Rebecca to be working on Christmas baskets in the novel. What ways does your family or church or community give back at Christmas?

4. Obviously, Lilly and Robert's story was a twist on O. Henry's famous story, "The Gift of the Magi." Have you ever had a Gift of the Magi moment, where you gave someone a gift that they couldn't use?

5. When I finished the novel, I still wasn't sure where Ben and Judith should live. Do you have a preference? Above the store like Gretta and Joshua? In Ben's house? Or, perhaps they need a new place of their own?

6. Is there a character in the Seasons of Sugarcreek novels who you would like to see more of? Why?

7. When I first read the Amish proverb, "The woods would be silent if only the best birds sang," I knew it would go well with this novel. Does the proverb resonate with you in any special way?

8. The following scripture verse helped me tremendously when writing this novel. Is there a person in your life who adds "light" to it? Can you think of a way that you add "light" to others?

"*When Jesus spoke again to the people, He said, 'I am the light of the world. Whoever follows me will never walk in darkness, but will have the light of life.'* "
John 8:12

Shelley Shepard Gray

© Mary Lou Zinsser

SHELLEY SHEPARD GRAY is the beloved author of the Sisters of the Heart series, including *Hidden*, *Wanted*, and *Forgiven*. Before writing, she was a teacher in both Texas and Colorado. She now writes full-time and lives in southern Ohio with her husband and two children. When not writing, Shelley volunteers at church, reads, and enjoys walking her miniature dachshund on her town's scenic bike trail.